DANGER

IN DEEP LAKE

DANGER

IN DEEP LAKE

GLORIA VAN

DEDICATION

To my amazing husband Onno, I give thanks for endless encouragement and love. You make life fun!

ACKNOWLEDGMENTS

Writing a novel – especially a first novel – is an exciting, scary, wonderful, daunting task. It is one I would never have tackled without the support and encouragement of many amazing people.

In the beginning, my dear friends Toni, Miki, Judy, Diane, and Gisela, insisted I do this project. I was then pushed and prodded and taught by M.J., Susan, and Crystal, who continued to support me to the end. Along the way, additional input was sought from Charlene, Ann, Diane, Karen, Judy, Toni, Greta, Steve, and Meg. Ruth and Jay gave wise advice on real estate, Steve gave first-hand information on NYC, and Bob gave me great information about bees and wasps.

To the incredible women of WOW (Women of Words) you know this wouldn't have happened without you.

My humble thanks go to all of you.

Gloria

CAST OF CHARACTERS

McKenzie (Kenzie) Ward, successful commercial real estate executive from New York, came back to Deep Lake, her hometown in Minnesota, at the death of her father.

James Archer Ward, McKenzie's father, and a former Minnesota judge, died in 2017 of wasp stings.

Rose Anne Weber Ward, McKenzie's mother who died in 2001.

William James Ward, McKenzie's older brother, who works at Ward Transport, owned by the family.

Dolly (Donna) Ward, William's wife.

Sophia Ward, William and Dolly's daughter, and McKenzie's niece.

Big Jim Ward, McKenzie's grandfather and owner of Ward Transport, who died in 1983.

Otis Jorgensen, Deputy Sheriff of Washington County and McKenzie's childhood friend.

Mary Jo (Hanson) Jorgensen, Otis's wife.

Al Jorgensen, Otis's father, and a house painter.

Nils Jorgensen (Gramps), Otis's grandfather.

Ed Johnson, long-time manager of Ward Transport, owned by the Ward family.

Michael Romano, NYC lawyer, boyfriend of McKenzie in New York.

Ethan Thompson, Deep Lake veterinarian, widower, and considered hot and eligible.

Isabella Thompson, five-year-old daughter of Ethan and her deceased mother, Elizabeth.

Janice Hopkins, friend of McKenzie's since high school, owns beauty shop in Deep Lake.

Vicky (Vidal) Vargas, Brazilian exchange student who stayed in Deep Lake after a gender change.

Desiree Canard, commercial realtor, and business partner of McKenzie in New York.

TABLE OF CONTENTS

PROLOGUE – 1992

Ten-year-old McKenzie Ward turned her head as she usually did when her best friend Otis suggested a spitting contest. It might be interesting to see how far they could spit a mouthful of water before it froze, but she had more important things on her mind.

After no positive response from Kenzie, Otis tried again. "Hey, after we win this contest, how about a good cowboy movie at Gramps'? Or we could throw stones off the trestle. Bet I can beat 'cha!"

They, and dozens of other eager kids had already climbed all over the city fire truck borrowed for the occasion. Kenzie and Otis were now sitting on two up-turned five-gallon buckets in front of a hole in the ice, waiting for the noon whistle blast from the fire truck to kick off the annual ice fishing contest on Deep Lake. The temperature that January day was a balmy three degrees Fahrenheit. Dressed in parkas, snow pants, and heavy boots, they had one short ice fishing pole between them, already rigged with one of Gramps' special hand-carved and hand–painted lures. Neither had any doubt that among the couple of hundred experienced adults and bunches of kids like themselves huddled around dozens of holes in the ice, the two of them would haul in the biggest walleye of the day.

There was a carnival atmosphere in the air, with laughter all around. There was also lots of stomping of feet in efforts to keep warm. Most of the adults were gathered around open holes in the ice and drinking something from steaming foam cups. Kids chased each other and skidded and slid in mock danger of getting too near the deep holes. Music played from battery operated boom boxes and poured from open-doored pickups scattered across the lake. With at least a foot of ice, driving on the frozen lake was not hazardous. Dozens of small fish-houses were placed strategically by veteran fisher-folk who spent many hours on the lake over the typical winter. Some of the fish-houses had small stoves in them for keeping occupants warm. They also had carpeting and padded benches, and always a card table in case a game came up with drop-in visitors.

The annual ice fishing contest was the big winter event in the small town of Deep Lake, Minnesota. Named after the extraordinarily deep lake it bordered, the town was northeast of the major Twin Cities of Minneapolis and St. Paul. Happily for its residents, the town had avoided becoming a bedroom community of commuters to the Twin Cities. Instead, it somehow remained a small town of farmers and serious fishermen who loved the many area lakes and streams. The one major industry was a pickle and jam factory on the edge of town that provided jobs but didn't distract much from the town's rural character.

The contest brought many visitors, but they never stayed long in the severe cold. Winter in northern Minnesota is something you have to grow up with to fully appreciate.

When the spitting challenge suggestion failed, Otis said, "Okay, how about ugly faces?"

"You're on," and Kenzie yanked off her mittens to pull her cheeks out in an open-mouthed grimace. They flapped their tongues at each other and rolled their eyes, trying not to laugh while also trying to look as ugly as they could.

"Fweeeeeeet!" screamed the whistle on the fire truck at noon on the dot, to signal the start of the fishing contest.

Kenzie and Otis grinned and blinked with ice-encrusted eyelashes, pulled on their puffy mittens and both yelled, "Dibs!"

Kenzie reached the pole first and dropped the hook-loaded lure into the frosty water at the bottom of the foot-thick hole. A spring bobber attached to the line smoothed out the jerkiness of jigging the swimming lure up and down and helped detect when fish took the bait.

Game on.

All over the lake noise abruptly stopped and fishing began in earnest. Prizes included a much-desired brand new snow-mobile with all the trimmings, plus a heavy-duty ice auger to more easily cut through the ice, lots of other fishing gear, and some hefty cash prizes, too. Hundreds of eyes peered into deep holes in the ice with greedy and anxious hope.

Twenty feet to the left of Kenzie and Otis someone heaved a medium-sized walleye onto the ice with a mighty roar. Also nearby, a kid they knew pulled in a tiny sunfish. Snickers drifted across the lake as others did the same thing.

Kenzie felt something touch her line. Fish are lethargic in the winter, so she wasn't surprised that it wasn't a hard hit. She jiggled the line and watched the bobber as it slowly sank under the water. Hanging over her shoulder, Otis grunted and Kenzie elbowed him out of her way. "I got something," she said. She started to pull in the line. "It feels weird – and heavy."

"Oh boy," mumbled Otis, "you've probably got a tree or an old tire or something. You shoulda let me be first."

Kenzie tore off her mittens and fell flat on the ice. She reached down into the hole to free her hook and grabbed what she thought might be a branch. She pulled it up through the hole and stared along with Otis at a brown and wrinkled human hand that laid there on the ice wrapped like a gift in her eight-pound fishing line. The arm it was attached to trailed back down into the dark and frigid water.

CHAPTER 1
TODAY

McKenzie Ward filed slowly off the plane at Minneapolis-St. Paul International Airport. The Boeing 737, the world's most popular passenger jet, had safely transported 162 visitors, vacationers, and businessmen and women from New York. Whether they arrived weary and bored or excited about upcoming adventures, every one of them had a story, and McKenzie was no exception. Hers was one of sadness and apprehension.

She had traveled to Minnesota to bury her father.

After picking up her rental car, McKenzie headed east on I-494, a road she hadn't traveled for almost half her lifetime. The surroundings became familiar as she passed the sprawling community of Woodbury, the turnoff to Lake Elmo, and White Bear Lake. The green almost overwhelmed her as she drove in summer's beauty through rolling hills covered with trees of every shade, and grasses waving. Farm fields were seen in the distance with crops lush and thriving. "Knee-high by the 4th of July," was the old saying for corn crops that farmers believed would ensure a productive yield, but with today's state-of-the-art farming methods and seeds, it was more like shoulder-high. Either way, the corn had met farmers' long-held criteria on this sun-filled July day, only a week after the 4th. After becoming I-694 as part of the interchange that circled the Twin Cities, the highway turned north. McKenzie slowed down to turn toward her childhood home in the village of Deep Lake.

Passing the family's trucking company, Ward Transport, memories overflowed as McKenzie slowly drove up Main Street. There was the old hamburger joint, updated to a supper club, and looking prosperous. The post office was still there, and the beauty and barber shops next to each other. It looked like unisex salons hadn't yet made it to Deep Lake. The library looked busy and reminded her of the time she and her old friend Otis got expelled from story time because they couldn't sit still; there were too many more exciting things to do outside. When the librarian sternly reprimanded them, they exploded out the door and went fishing.

Creeks abounded in the town of Deep Lake, some quiet and gentle with only a trickle making its way to the lake, and others were stretched to their banks with gurgling rapids. Water was plentiful in all of Washington County, and young Kenzie and Otis caught every kind of fish. Lying on their bellies, they watched the crawdads and tadpoles. They caught frogs and toads and had jumping contests. The state is called "The land of 10,000 lakes." McKenzie remembered her school report how Minnesota actually had 11,842 lakes larger than ten acres.

McKenzie was a tomboy who would rather go fishing or look for creepy things with best pal Otis. They rode their bikes around the town and knew absolutely everything that went on. They would hide behind trees and watch when anything exciting and sometimes not so exciting happened in the town.

One time there was a strange man who lived in the basement of the building next to the post office. He was scary at first, but one day he fixed Otis's bicycle, and they got to be friends. Otis told McKenzie about the time he went down into his basement where the man, called Wheelie because of his fascination for wheels, had dozens of wheels in every size. He used them to make odd toys and sculptures with moving parts. Otis was spellbound by the huge contraption of tiny wheels and spools and other moving devices that circled the basement. When Wheelie touched one piece, the whole structure started to move until the entire sculpture was in motion. Then there was the day Wheelie went berserk and started shooting a gun from his basement window. McKenzie and Otis watched it all from across the street behind a tree as the sheriff and many local townsmen shot back and eventually killed Wheelie. No one knew what triggered the shooting or what had snapped in Wheelie's mind that day. McKenzie had never been brave enough to follow Otis into Wheelie's basement, but she shared the sadness at his terrible and mysterious end.

Trying unsuccessfully to push nostalgia aside, McKenzie turned around and went back down Main Street to Deep Lake Road. She turned onto Maple Street and pulled up in front of her childhood home.

The house looked the same as always, big, white, and solid. Like clockwork on standing orders, her friend Otis's father, Al Jorgensen, had painted the Ward house every ten years, inside and out, always the same colors; white outside, eggshell inside. Lugging buckets and ladders and drop cloths, McKenzie could still hear him tunelessly humming his way around her house. When they were really young, she and Otis hid under cloth-covered tables and made forts and hidey-holes and ran their little toy cars dangerously close to the paint cans. Their only reprimand a quiet, "Not too close, kids," and Al went back to his humming.

The street was aptly named, with towering Sugar Maples along the boulevard. The two in front of the house brought back a memory, sweet and stinging at the same time. McKenzie remembered her mother planting the tiny seedlings almost thirty years before. Very young then, she helped her mother dig the holes; Kenzie with a small plastic shovel and her mother wielding a heavy-duty spade. Covered with dirt and sweat, with smiles of accomplishment for both of them, her mother said, "Someday these trees will be majestic, not just taller than you or me, but even taller than the house. Just you wait." She was right.

"Oh Mom, I still miss you so much," McKenzie cried out loud. Her mind filled with visions of her mother smiling, frowning, laughing, yelling. "I want to hear you curse in your own special way."

When McKenzie and Otis were growing up, Rose Ward, a gentle, kind, and soft-spoken woman who loved all kinds of flowers, would occasionally let out a frustrated curse using names of weeds. "Oh thistle!" she would say under her breath when she hit her thumb or accidentally cut a finger. "You're acting like crabgrass!" Rose would pseudo-shout at the two of them when they tracked in mud from the creek or emptied their pockets filled with bugs and every sort of creature.

The worst they could earn was "Oh pigweed!" in the most disgusting tone of voice they had ever heard, making them wonder if they'd ever be forgiven in this lifetime. Only once did she use that one on Kenzie and Otis, and the memory was burned into her mind. Kindergarteners, they loved painting pictures at school. One day, they discovered the spice cupboard at Kenzie's house and poured some of the dry spices out on the floor. They experimented a little and found that mixed with a little water, some of the spices made wonderful colors like the paints they used at school. Making little cups of "paint," just like Otis's dad, they drew pictures on the kitchen walls. Turmeric and curry made bright yellow flowers, parsley made green trees, and paprika was perfect for red.

When they called Rose in to see their beautiful handiwork, she gasped, "Oh pigweed!" They didn't know the dyes were permanent; they were proud of their stunning artwork. Al had to make an unscheduled repainting of the kitchen the next week, using several coats of stain-killer, and Otis didn't come over for a couple of days.

Her mother's funeral in 2001, was the last time McKenzie had been back to Deep Lake. And, sadly, she was there again, to bury her father, in 2017.

James Archer Ward was a good man. Tall and broad, James, as he was always called, was the type of man who filled a room when he entered it. His deep voice and direct gaze made people come to attention when he spoke. From the time she was small, McKenzie noticed that when her daddy said something, everyone listened.

James' father, Big Jim Ward, had run the trucking company he owned until his death in 1983. James had already chosen the law and didn't want to work with the trucking company, so for several years, Big Jim's young protégé, Ed Johnson, had worked with him. When Big Jim became elderly and ill, he pretty much turned the company over to Ed to run, and Ed was still at the helm of the company.

After watching James's youth filled with serious study and an almost unnatural attention to legal matters, Big Jim agreed that James's life would not be fulfilled by running an LTL trucking company that hauled Less-Than-Truckload goods around the Twin Cities. Instead, James went to what was then the William Mitchell College of Law in St. Paul, Minnesota, and excelled in his studies. After many years of a successful law practice in Deep Lake, he was appointed a Minnesota Tenth District Judge in 1996 by Governor Arne Carlson. He was reelected every six years until forced to retire at age seventy.

James was seventy-five on his last birthday, too young to be gone. McKenzie was still in shock from the phone call from her uncle Archie telling her of her father's death. By wasp sting, of all things. McKenzie knew about her dad's allergy to insect venom, a worrisome thing when you considered all the time he spent fishing or hunting or just being out of doors. He always carried an Epi-pen and Benadryl in case he got stung, which he did on occasion, but a shot at the ER and a course of steroids usually took care of it and he always seemed so strong. Dying of a wasp sting was something she couldn't have dreamed was a possibility.

McKenzie was still sitting in her rental car at the curb while memories flooded her mind when a car pulled up beside hers. A tall, starkly uniformed man appeared at her window. She lowered the window as he gaped at her saying, "Well, look what the cat dragged in! I thought I had a stalker here, parked on a side street and watching the houses."

"Otis!"

McKenzie leaped out of the car and into his arms. She blinked a tear away as Otis drew her close for a fierce hug and a rumbled greeting. His boyish face had matured, and he was a strong-looking handsome man, with short dark blond hair, and a wide smile.

"It's been way too long, buddy. But I knew for sure you'd show up this time."

"I couldn't come before, Otis. I just couldn't."

"Yeah, yeah…"

"Hey, are you the sheriff now?"

"No, but I'm a sheriff's deputy. I run the office here in Deep Lake for Washington County – have for a few years now. We're not big enough for a police department, so I'm sort of what there is. Plus, there's one other guy who helps bring in the drunks and keep things in order. You know I always wanted to work in law enforcement, and I hope to be sheriff one day."

"Yes, Dad did keep me in the loop. He also mentioned you got married."

"I did – to Mary Jo Hanson. She was a few grades behind us and you might remember her. I don't know how I got lucky enough to be the one she wanted. We've got two amazing young ones now, but let's catch up later. I want to hear everything about what you've been up to and I could talk for hours about my boys."

*****

Otis now looked more watchfully at McKenzie. She was a natural beauty as he always knew she'd turn out to be, tall and blond and lithe. Beyond that, he began to see the old Kenzie, as he always called her. He also saw her hesitancy to enter the house, and he knew she didn't want to go in alone. He offered, "Let's go see how things look in the house. Your dad went so quickly, nobody has been here for a few days."

"What really happened? Please tell me."

"You need to know that I checked everything out at the scene of his death as carefully as I could. It looks like your dad was getting ready to fish and was taking out his tackle box from the back of his car. In fact, he was meeting Jake Connor at the lower end of Lake Elmo, one of their favorite fishing holes. James got there a little early. I've looked at the situation with other law enforcement people, including our sheriff, a dozen times, and we can't find where the wasps came from. It could have been that he parked too close to their nest or spooked a swarm somehow as he opened the hatch-back. I've been talking with a couple of beekeepers in the area who know about the habits of wasps, but we haven't been able to come up with an answer yet. We're still looking, but we might never know. He was stung at least twenty times in a frenzied attack, and he never had the chance to get to his Epi-pen that was in the arm-rest compartment of his car, only a few feet away. When Jake got there, it was already over, and James was dead."

"Poor Dad. I talked to him a couple of weeks ago and he sounded so strong, just like always. I was actually thinking of coming for a visit soon. He sounded a little contemplative and said something about the trucking company maybe having some changes. I was thinking it was time for me to come home to see him."

He took her arm and they walked up the curved sidewalk edged in perennials which her mother had planted many years before.

"Believe it or not, I'm pretty tough these days," Kenzie confided. "But stepping back into Deep Lake … makes me feel like a vulnerable young girl again."

"That ain't all bad. We had a blast back then. Remember the time we were slogging around in the creek and went back to your place? Your mom was waiting at the door with her knowing smirk. One look at your turtle and the salamander hanging out of my pocket and she was sure we were out to scare the dog!"

"The dog. I know old Goldie died years ago. Dad mentioned getting another dog a while ago and said it was a comfort to him. We never talked much about what he did from day to day, in fact. I'm feeling more and more guilty about neglecting him for so long because about all we did was exchange niceties. I really believe the hurting was so bad for both of us after Mom's terrible death, that we couldn't bridge that gap."

Otis was silent for a moment as they both collected their thoughts, and continued, "He did have a dog. In fact, he got another Golden a few years ago and named her Goldie 2. Your family always liked the retrievers, and I know you'll like this one. She's over at your brother's now, but I don't think Dolly likes her much. Hair and dirt and all … maybe now you're here you can bring her home for a while."

*****

"My brother. Do you see much of Will? How is he doing?" McKenzie's six-year-older brother William was not her favorite person, nor had he ever been. She never understood frankly, how William was ever born to her brilliant father and saintly mother. Good-looking but lazy and arrogant, he was a football star for a while in high school, but he burned out by senior year because it was a lot of work and work just wasn't his thing. William had cheated his way through high school and quickly flunked out of Carleton, the prestigious top liberal arts college he insisted on attending.

"Well, he hasn't changed much. I guess that's all I'll say for now. Let's go in the house."

They had walked around the back and using the key above the back door, they let themselves into the kitchen. Everything looked the same. There was a new countertop, and a few new appliances, but the same egg shell walls. Memories engulfed her. She knew what every cupboard contained, and when she opened a door just to be sure, the cups were hanging from the same hooks.

The house was clean and neat, just the way her parents lived. Every piece of furniture was where it had been sixteen years before. Pictures of her grandparents and other family members hung where they always did. The beautiful painting of the Minnesota north woods, a gift from her father's former law partner, enhanced the living room, along with the framed wood-burning of the judge fly-fishing. Her father had commissioned a picture by a young artist who couldn't afford paints. Instead, she used birch wood bark and wood-burned the image onto it, creating a precious work of art.

Otis offered, "Hey, I think I still see the outline of our orange flowers on the kitchen wall. Do you think she's still swearing at us in heaven?" Obviously, the memory of that day was burned into his mind, as it was in hers.

"Oh pigweed, it feels so good to be here now!" McKenzie felt the presence of her mother and could see her dad in his fly-fishing gear as he prepared to go out to catch the "smallies," as he called his favorite smallmouth bass. He spent more time at the Fly Shop in Lake Elmo than he did at home on summer weekends, just shooting the breeze with fellow fishermen.

Her father was meticulous in maintaining the huge house built in the 1850s, but McKenzie thought, with a stab in her heart, why didn't he do a better job of maintaining the wiring? Her mother had died horribly and uselessly, in the upstairs bathtub. An old radio had always stood on a shelf above the tub, and the new wiring that prevented accidents like that had never been installed. That day, with Rose relaxing in the tub listening to her favorite show tunes on the radio, it fell into the tub and she was electrocuted.

CHAPTER 2
1992

The sheriff had arrived along with several other official-looking individuals. Kenzie and Otis peered around the side of a fish house near by where they had run after being shooed away from the sight they were told they were too young to witness. The officials were stringing red tape that said "danger," all around the area, and the ice-fishing contest was pretty much done for. The crowds were held back but there was a lot of chatter going on and people kept inching closer to see what was happening.

Otis and Kenzie had already been questioned briefly by the sheriff but were told they had to go to the deputy's office the next day to give further "statements."

The sheriff had brought a bigger auger. They enlarged the hole and hauled the body up through it. It was spread out on the ice and the county coroner who came from Stillwater was bending over it.

"What's a statement, Otis?" Kenzie asked nervously. "I thought all we had to do was tell them what happened."

"Beats me. I sure hope your dad will go with us. This is scary." They hunkered down and watched the coroner study the naked body.

"I think he could have been in the water for a long time. That skin is like leather, but he's so well-preserved, it's hard to tell. His clothes are gone, but look here – there's a rotted piece of rope on his ankle. What do you make of that, Jack?" the coroner asked the sheriff.

"Damned if I know, Bill. Let's get him back to your lab so you can get this figured out and we can find out who he is. Besides, the natives are getting restless here and we need to clear this mess up."

Kenzie and Otis decided there was no more to see, so they ran as fast as they could back to Otis's house to tell Gramps all about what happened.

Nils Jorgensen was Otis's grandfather and everyone called him Gramps. After his wife Astrid died, Gramps moved in with Otis's family, across the alley from McKenzie's house. Gramps had been a baker and ran Deep Lake's bakery shop, "Bread and Norske Treats." He and Astrid had run the bakery for many years until it was time to retire. Their older son Sven and his wife took it over and still ran it.

Gramps still baked great bread and Otis's mom, Millie, happily turned over her kitchen to Gramps when he was in the mood to bake. It was a special day when Kenzie and Otis walked through the back door to the smell of baking bread. Gramps also made sweet fried fattigman, and his lefse was unbeatable.

Puffing from their run, Kenzie and Otis burst through the kitchen door, yelling, "Gramps! Gramps! You're not gonna believe what happened!"

"Hold it now, you scalawags – what's the big rush?" said Gramps from his recliner in the living room where he had been sneaking a snooze.

"The fishing contest … hole in the ice … a hand … the sheriff," Kenzie and Otis talked over each other in their exhilaration.

"Whoa there – one at a time!" Gramps sat up in anticipation.

Otis shouted louder and gained Gramps' ear. "We hooked a body, Gramps! A real live dead body in the lake!"

The full story came tumbling out and soon the kids were exhausted by the telling. Gramps was wide awake by that time and well aware of the seriousness of what they were saying. He decided to distract them from their gruesome story by offering some cookies and milk, and all of them tramped off in search of the sandbakkels Gramps had made earlier.

After the cookies, when Otis and Kenzie ran out the back door to tell their friends about their surprising catch, Gramps picked up the phone to call the sheriff.

CHAPTER 3
TODAY

Back outside the house, Otis and Kenzie tried briefly to catch up for the past sixteen years.

"So, from what your dad said, you've done pretty well in the big city," said Otis. Inside, he was thinking how slick she looked. Blond hair that fell exactly right from a pricey haircut, a pant-suit that definitely didn't come from J.C. Penny's, with her all-together beauty fit snugly inside it. Maybe she's a runner now, he guessed as he unconsciously sucked in his gut that was hardly beginning to show. Oh hell, it was just so good to see Kenzie again – who cared how they looked?

"Yeah, I've done okay, I guess," she remarked. "Once I really got into commercial real estate after college, it just seemed to take off. It was so hard when Mom died. I went back to New York after her funeral and just dug in my heels. It seemed like it was all I could do to hold myself together and work seemed to dull the pain. Deep Lake just fell away and the harder I worked the easier it was to make myself forget."

They were interrupted by Kenzie's cell phone beeping. A message had come in, but she didn't even glance at it.

"I never heard if you got married, but your dad surely would have said something. You got a boyfriend out there?"

"Yes, I do have someone. Actually, we're sort of engaged now."

"Sort of? What's that mean?" It sounded to Otis like Kenzie was trying to convince herself.

Suddenly all business, Kenzie said, "I should check that message, Otis. I'm going to bring in my things from the car. Looks like I'll be staying here for a few days at least. We can catch up later."

"Sure, I'll help you."

After carrying in Kenzie's sleek matching luggage, Otis said, "How about a cup of coffee later at Joe's? It's still where it always was – the place where everyone goes for breakfast after church on Sundays. Remember when we used to share a hot fudge malt and drive everyone nuts when we slurped the bottom of the can with our straws?"

"Oh, do I! That's a taste you never forget. Too many calories to think about these days. See you there about four?"

"Works for me. Can you make time for supper at our house tomorrow night? Mary Jo's a great cook and she would love to have you come. I can't wait for you to meet her and you're going to love my little guys. We're just over on Elm; I'll text you the address."

"Great – see you at four."

Leaving her luggage in the front hall, McKenzie checked a text from her friend Michael. Short and blunt, it said only, "Call me." She decided to deal with it later.

McKenzie wandered through the old house and the longer she was there, the more comfortable she felt. It was good to be home again after so long away. She ran her hand over the nicely kept woodwork of the beautiful stairway to the second floor. Her father obviously still had someone come in to clean once a week or so. Old Clara must be long gone by now, but memories of the cantankerous Clara flooded her mind. She and

Otis were often the brunt of her rantings about bringing in dirt, and she would literally sweep them out the door with her ever-present broom, yelling at them in her native Czech tongue.

The house was quiet now, but memories flashed in McKenzie's mind. Her father had aluminum windows installed in the fifteen-room house to replace the old kind that needed storms and screens put up each fall and spring. She remembered there were fifty-two windows in the house including all those in the porches. There was one really little one in what they called the mini-bath near the kitchen. Old Clara said they should have just covered that window with a Band-Aid because it was so small, instead of spending the money for a fancy window.

The front stairway started in what they always called the music room because that's where the piano had always been, and it was still there, she noted. She took many lessons on that piano, but she hadn't touched a piano of any kind for longer than she could remember.

The room was a large vestibule or entry area inside the front door, lit by a huge chandelier with crystals hanging from it. Many early mornings McKenzie sat on the landing of the stairway watching rainbows fly around the room as the beveled crystals gently moved in the sun. Her mother said when you saw rainbows in a room, it meant angels were saying hello. Many curious conversations were held with these mysterious angels as McKenzie watched the rainbows from her perch on the stair landing. The last angel talk was accompanied by endless tears as she sat in this very spot mourning her mother after coming back from being away at college for only two months.

Upstairs, her room was exactly as it was when she left for college sixteen years before. A poster of Janet and Michael Jackson was next to the bed. She glanced at the framed photos on the wall of McKenzie and her girlfriends, McKenzie and Otis, McKenzie and her family. Gazing thoughtfully at her parents, she saw her brother William between her and her mother. He was pinching McKenzie's arm really hard when the picture was taken and her smile was contorted, while his was just plain creepy.

William. She was not eager to see him even after all the years she'd been away. At the same time, she felt guilty about being reluctant to see him. She wondered how he was coping with their father's death and how it would change their lives.

In spite of her apprehensions about the funeral and dealing with William, she was unexpectedly comforted by being in this wonderful old house. It felt so right. It was comfort she hadn't felt in too long a time.

CHAPTER 4
1992

Reaching his long-time friend, Sheriff Jack Benson, Gramps said, "Sounds like you had some excitement at the fishing contest, Jack."

"If that's what you want to call it, I guess so, Nils. What a day!"

"Know who it is yet?"

"No. The coroner is working on it. The body's in odd shape – really leathery skin and nobody can tell how long he's been in the water. I'm working now on trying to find out about missing men in the area. You know things like this happen all the time in the Cities, but not out here for God's sake! That girl of James's just hauled that body up like it was a walleye. She's got spunk, that kid."

"The kids were pretty wound up about the whole thing – scared at first, but like ten-year-olds, once they got it all out they went out to tell their friends. They still have to give you a statement?"

"Yeah. I told them to come in tomorrow and I think Otis's dad and James will come with them. They don't need a lawyer of course, but her dad needs to be there. McKenzie said he wasn't at the fishing contest because he had some legal business – even on a Sunday. Does he know yet?"

"I'm going to call him now, but I expect he knows already – the whole town will be buzzing from all of this. How about the media – they giving you any trouble?"

"No. I gave them a statement to use for TV and the papers. I told them the kids were off limits. Make sure they don't bug 'em, okay?"

"Will do, Jack. I'll call James now to be sure he's got the story as we know it. Lotta turmoil for our little town."

*****

The Coroner, Bill Engebretsen, had done all he could in an autopsy of the body McKenzie and Otis hauled up from the lake. He had called the sheriff and the two of them were talking it over while looking at the leathery-skinned body lying on the autopsy table.

"Jack, this body has been in the water for a long time. It's not someone who recently went missing. In fact, this may be hard for you to believe, but I've been doing some research on how water can preserve a body. I hate to bore you, but I'll start with some of the facts I learned."

"Go ahead, Bill, I'm all ears."

"The Minnesota Department of Natural Resources gave me more accurate information than I remembered from geography when I was a kid. We all know the Great Lakes and the lakes in Minnesota were formed when glaciers receded during the last ice age. They say it was about 15,000 years ago when glaciers retreated and spread over the landscape, carving out holes and leaving behind ice chunks. As these ice chunks melted in the holes left behind, lakes were formed, called kettle lakes.

"While Lake Superior has a maximum depth of 1,290 feet, most of the lakes in Minnesota are only about 30 to 40 feet deep or less on average, but there are some that go down about 200 feet and more. We know that our Deep Lake has a really deep hole at the north end, while the south part of the lake is much shallower. The hole could go as far down as 140-150 feet, which must have been a really heavy chunk of ice at one time. Given our winter temperatures around here, the water at that depth is never much above freezing."

"Yeah, I know most of this stuff, too, but I like the way you're putting it together. Keep going."

"What I've concluded from my research is this. It seems that the perfect combination of pressure, oxygen, and cold temperature at extreme lake depth can mummify and preserve a body. By accident or on purpose, the deep hole at the north end of Deep Lake is exactly where this body went down.

"What I've found in the autopsy is that this guy was in good health and in his mid-twenties or so according to my results. Unfortunately, he was shot twice in the back of the head, which is what killed him. He was then tied to something heavy and thrown into the lake at just the right place. His clothes have rotted away, and apparently, the rope used to tie him to something heavy also rotted and that's why he finally floated up to the surface."

"Oh man, this is great!" exclaimed the sheriff. "So that's how the Ward kid was able to snag him. What do we do next?"

"Well, the beauty of all this is that the body was basically mummified and we can obtain actual fingerprints that can identify him. I have to do some work to get the fingerprints. Then we need to work with the FBI because they manage all the fingerprint sets collected in the U.S., as you know, and that's where you come in, Jack. By the way, they started fingerprinting around 1912 or so, and I think this guy may go back almost as far as that."

"No kidding! I'll get on it as soon as you can get me some prints. What's your guess, as to how long he's been in the water?"

"Good question. I'm making a pretty good guestimate here because of the condition of the body, and the execution-style bullet holes in his head. And, one thing I didn't tell you is that I've got the bullets, too. I found out they're from a Colt M1911 .38 Super, an automatic pistol. Did a little research here, too, and I learned from 1929 until the .357 Magnum appeared in 1934, the .38 Super was the fastest pistol bullet, something every self-respecting gangster appreciated."

"Are you saying this was a gangster killing?"

"It sure looks like it could be from the bullets I recovered from this guy's skull. You need to look at them, too, because you know more about that stuff than I do. My guess is that we should look at a gangster killing from the early 1930s. If you agree, that's where I think we should start when we get the fingerprints submitted to the FBI."

"Wow, this is mind-blowing! Let's get busy and find out who this guy was!"

*****

Several weeks went by while the coroner and the sheriff did their work with the FBI. They were elated that the fingerprinting worked, and the body was positively identified. Sheriff Benson called James Ward and asked to meet with him to talk about what had developed. They were sitting over coffee at Joe's restaurant.

"James, thanks for seeing me today. Bill Engebretsen has done a fine job of providing the information needed to identify the man your daughter pulled out of the lake."

"That's great, Jack, and I'm glad to do what I can, but what does this have to do with me?"

"Well, it's sort of a long story. It's a lot of research and may sound boring, but it's all connected and it's important that you hear it."

"Well, I'm eager to hear it – go ahead and let her fly."

"We discovered the man was an active gangster in the 1930s. He was involved in a bank robbery over in Hudson, Wisconsin. You know how St. Paul was a sanctuary for criminals in the Midwest. They had the support of corrupt politicians and even the police chief who turned a blind eye to smuggling, racketeering, prostitution, and gambling.

"As you may already know, it started in 1900. There was an unwritten sort of contract between gangsters and Chief of Police, John O'Connor. This contract meant criminals could stay in the city under three conditions: that they checked in with police when they arrived, they agreed to pay bribes from their profits to city officials, and they committed no major crimes in the city of St. Paul."

"Yes, you're right on that. I remember that Minneapolis was fair game, but the O'Connor Layover Agreement, that's what they called it, protected St. Paul. This contract lasted for almost forty years until the feds and local crusaders stepped in to end it."

Jack continued, "Of course, Prohibition from 1919 to 1933 opened up all new and very lucrative avenues with bootlegging, smuggling, and illegal sale of alcohol when breweries and distilleries closed. And can you believe it was a Minnesota congressman who put the enforcement mechanism in place for it? It was called The Volstead Act, or the National Prohibition Act, and St. Paul became known as one of the 'wettest' cities in the nation.

"Many notorious criminals felt perfectly safe in St. Paul and stayed in the city, especially when the heat was on and they needed a place to lay low for a while. Even Al 'Scarface' Capone stayed here. Clyde Barrow and Bonnie Parker looked for protection in St. Paul while committing their crimes in other Midwestern areas. John Dillinger and his girlfriend Evelyn Frechette had an apartment in St. Paul for a while and had a shoot-out with a rookie FBI agent one time. And that's why I'm telling you all of this. We believe John Dillinger may have been involved in the bank robbery in Hudson along with our guy from the lake.

"Now, we don't know all the details of what happened, but we've been checking the newspaper articles from the day and Bill has really grabbed this thing by the horns and done a hell of a good job of research. From everything he's found out, he believes that Antonio Antonini, the guy in the lake ..."

Listening patiently and nodding now and then through Jack's discourse, James suddenly interrupted, "Wait a minute. Antonio Antonini? I remember that name – he's the guy who owned the trucking company my father bought!"

"You got it, that's the guy. Bill has figured out that Antonini supplied the van for the Hudson job. Not only did he supply the truck, he drove it as the getaway vehicle. He was doing some illegal hauling of some kind with his trucks – might have been booze, but we don't know how he graduated to working with John Dillinger.

"Something must have gone wrong in the robbery and somehow Antonini was shot and dumped in Deep Lake. Bad as that sounds, it happened a lot in those days. Bodies were found in lakes and ponds all over the eastern suburbs of St. Paul in the 1930s. I'm afraid we'll never know why this one was dumped in the deep spot and never found until nearly sixty years later."

"This is a lot to take in, Jack. I have to think about how Dad got the company from Antonini. From what I remember, the company came on the market about that time. I'll do some digging in the files – Dad kept everything, you know, so it's gotta be there somewhere. I'll get back to you as soon as I can find what I need. Okay with you?"

"Certainly. We haven't found any next of kin for Antonini, and we're not sure if he had any family. He'll likely be cremated and buried in what stands for "boot hill" now, a portion of our Deep Lake Cemetery. At least he'll have a name on his grave, bad guy that he was."

*****

James canceled his afternoon appointments and went immediately to Ward Transport to see Ed Johnson, who had been running the company since James, Sr. died in 1983. "Hey Ed, good to see you," shaking his hand.

"Yes, same here. What brings you over here, James, I haven't heard from you for a while?"

"Well, you're doing such a good job of taking care of things, I don't need to come by often. Today, I've got a bit of a problem. I need to do some rummaging in my dad's old papers. It has to do with how Dad bought the company originally. I think it was in 1936 or so, but I need to see what he has for papers on the deal."

"I've got all of his papers in the back room. I hated to throw any of it away without your going through things, so I just boxed it all up. You're welcome to look through it. I hope you find what you need," Ed said as they walked toward the back of the office.

Opening the door, they looked in at a huge pile of boxes, but Ed had dated each one as carefully as he was able. James gave a big sigh, "Got any coffee?"

Ed laughed, "Sure, I think you might be needing some, be right back with it. Good luck."

James started his search and found himself immersed in memories as he sorted through his father's well-organized paperwork of so many years. He found a box labeled 1936 and opened the cover. His dad was only twenty-four years old when he started the business, and the first thing James saw was a picture of his dad, Big Jim, as his father had been known, not just because of his height, but he was broad and strong. He was shown shaking hands with a small, thin, and solemn bearded gentleman in front of the Deep Lake Bank. Big Jim was smiling widely. "Well, that's a good sign," James thought to himself.

Digging further, he came across the deed to the company itself. It appeared that the trucking company had been abandoned in 1934, and all the employees left. A cement block building was still standing at the time, and there were a couple of old trucks. No one knew what happened to the owner, Antonio Antonini, who had disappeared with no trace. Nothing was known about any family or relatives. Antonini had stopped making payments on the company and equipment. Eventually, the bank took possession.

Big Jim had written the story in his own cramped hand with questionable spelling, but it was priceless to James when he discovered the precious journal. As his father told the story, no one in the area wanted to take over the abandoned business or pay the bank's price for a couple of years, until young Jim Ward happened by it one day. He was looking for something just like this, having escaped his father's farm as a younger son. His older brother wanted to take over the farm, which was fine with him, and in 1936 he was curious about this transportation business. It could be fun and it might even make him some money down the line. He had saved what he could by working on neighboring farms since he graduated from eighth grade, and never spent much. He thought he just might be able to make this work.

Big Jim came up with enough money as a down payment to satisfy the bank, and they gave him a reasonable loan to buy the company. Ward Transport was begun.

James wiped his eyes as he looked again at the photo and the happy smile on his father's face. What a joyous day that must have been for him.

CHAPTER 5
TODAY

Sighing, McKenzie stowed her bag in her old room and curled up on the bed with a pang for old times. She pulled out her cell phone and looked at Michael's message again. It seemed out of place. Even looking at a cell phone felt odd in these surroundings. Instead of calling, she texted him back: "Arrived OK, more later." It somehow felt good to be as blunt as his message had been to her.

With memories swirling in her brain, she gave in to a nagging headache and closed her eyes.

Waking with a start, she was disoriented and confused about where she was. Reality hit with a thud, and she was overwhelmed by grief. Yes, she was there to bury her father, but it became clear that it was her mother she missed the most. "Oh Mom, what really happened on that terrible day?"

Checking her watch, it was already almost four. She quickly unpacked and stowed her clothes in the nearly-empty closet. Seeing the clothes she wore as a teenager showed clearly that clothes hadn't been very important to her as a kid, and they didn't seem to be now either, she thought curiously. However, it was satisfying to discover that her old clothes still fit. Donning some comfy jeans she headed off to meet Otis at Joe's.

Gone was the bell that used to tinkle when anyone walked in the door. Some new booths had been added and things had been moved around, but it still felt like the same old Joe's. Joe himself greeted her, "So sorry to hear about your dad, McKenzie. He was a good man and he will be missed in Deep Lake."

"Thanks, Joe, that's good to hear."

She saw Otis already with a double hot-fudge malt in front of him, both the tall tulip glass and the can holding the second half. There were two spoons and straws. "I knew you really wanted this but would only order coffee. It's time to indulge."

"You were right – gimme my straw!" and she grabbed the can. "I've waited sixteen years for this!" Relishing the never-forgotten taste, she continued, "Sorry I was a little late; a nap sneaked up on me. I can't remember the last time I've actually taken a nap. Seems like all my defenses left me the moment I got back to this town." McKenzie slowed her slurping as a little brain-freeze took over from the ice-cold malt. "Sheeyit, this tastes so good!"

Otis quietly watched and grinned at his old friend. "It's so great to see you looking – and sounding – a little more normal. Tell me about your big-city life. Are you really as successful as your dad said you were?"

"Yeah, things have gone pretty well for me there. Commercial real estate was and still is booming. I managed to be at the right place at the right time. It wasn't easy, but I guess I had the fire in my belly, as they say. Every time a challenge came up, I just dove in. I took a lot of risks – like buying a building in Manhattan when I didn't have the cents or the sense, but then I thought about my mom and there wasn't a choice anymore. I just did it."

"Sounds like you work way too hard. Don't you ever kick loose like you used to? What about this 'sort of' fiancé? Is he up for some tadpoling up the creek?" Otis wiggled his brows a little.

"No, Michael isn't the tadpole type. But to be fair to him, I got caught up in my work a long time ago and he fits well into that lifestyle. He's a lawyer, handles many of my commercial deals. Honestly, sometimes it feels like the work never stops."

"Tell me you have some fun."

"Hmmm, fun. I haven't thought about fun for a while. I go to plays and concerts, and a lot of dinners … Fun. I have to think about that. What do you do for fun here in Deep Lake? It hasn't changed all that much. There can't be that much to do here."

"Well, just being married to Mary Jo is fun by itself. Our two boys keep us on the run 24/7, but we sneak off for dinner together once in a while – there are some great places in Stillwater. We go camping and take trips in our small camper. We're planning a trip out to the Black Hills later this summer when the boys are done with baseball and swimming lessons.

"My folks still live just a block over on Spruce. Gramps moved in with them after Grandma Jorgensen died. It's just Mom and Dad there now, and they love to watch the boys for us once in a while so we can get away. Dad's pretty much retired from house painting now, but drags out his brushes for one of our rooms when we really need help."

McKenzie sounded wistful, "Your camping trip sounds like a dream to me. I can't even imagine myself in that sort of scenario. The closest I get to nature is running every morning I can find time for it in Central Park. It sounds good, but about a million others do the same thing and it's like joining a herd. You have to wait till there's a break in the crowd before you can even jump in. Everybody's in their own world, sweating and gulping from their designer water bottles, eager to get it done so they can start their work day. It keeps me healthy, but I can't say it feels like fun."

Otis shook his head with thoughtful disapproval then moved on. "The funeral's on Thursday. Being today's Monday, that doesn't give you a lot of time. Need help with anything?"

"Dad had everything pretty well organized. I guess when Mom died, he bought some sort of policy that prepaid everything for his own funeral. He arranged it all with John and Lynn back then, from the music to the flowers. I trust them, of course. They've been in the business a long time. It's just a matter of my showing up, apparently. So, are their kids taking over the business?"

"Yeah, they've expanded with more funeral homes around the area. That business has changed along with everything else these days. They do more cremations now. I expect John and Lynn will retire soon – Holmes Funeral Homes will be around for a while yet, and their kids are doing a good job of it already."

"I do have to see Dad's attorney, Dave Manson. There's a formal 'reading of the will' Wednesday morning at his old law partner's office. Don't know why it has to be formal, but that's what Dave told me. William and I have to be there at ten o'clock sharp."

"Speaking of William – are you going to see your brother before then?"

"Yes, I'd better call him today. You mentioned there's a dog. Maybe it would be good if I offered to take care of it while I'm here. It might help things with his wife, but I expect Dolly doesn't like me anymore now than she ever did."

"Dolly will never change. She doesn't like the dog, which is a 'she' by the way, and a beauty. Looks just like Goldie, the Golden Retriever you used to have and I know you'll be hooked the minute you see her. There's dog food at the house and she won't be a bother. I've gotta run. I have to pick up one of the boys and Mary Jo will be expecting me home for supper. Plan on supper at our house tomorrow night about six. You do know that I inherited the Jorgensen house, don't you? I never did get very far from my roots, and we're living in what I always think of as Gramp's house just a block over on Elm. You certainly know the way. Oh, you're not on one of these no-gluten, sugar-free, cardboard-only diets, are you? Mary Jo is a great cook, and she'll accommodate with whatever you like."

Kenzie laughed. "Hey, this is home! Tell her to bring on the good stuff!"

"See ya then. Good luck with William."

Both headed out to their cars after Otis paid the bill. The restaurant had cleared out to get ready for the supper crowd, but there were still several heads turning to see who was the pretty woman laughing with Otis.

CHAPTER 6
TUESDAY MORNING

The night in her childhood room was surprisingly calming. Evening and morning rituals felt comfortable and natural, and McKenzie found herself wandering around the big house and remembering happy times with her family. She had stopped at the local grocery store the night before to get supplies for a week or so. As she chewed her favorite cereal with the morning sun shining through the window, she was wearing a grin.

Calling her brother was at the top of her to-do list. She had avoided it the night before. It just felt so good to be there with her memories and the house was so welcoming. Her evening was quiet and relaxing, a combination she hadn't enjoyed for a long time. She didn't want to spoil it by talking to William. Now, with a sigh, she picked up the phone in the kitchen and dialed William's number which was taped to the wall next to the phone. "Thanks, Dad, for the list," she whispered.

William answered with a curt, "Ward."

"Hello Will, it's McKenzie."

"It's about time. I've been waiting to hear from you." Blunt and direct, William hadn't changed.

"I just got in yesterday. Sorry I haven't called before this." McKenzie unconsciously reverted to her long-ago intimidated response. That had always been the norm for conversations with her bullying brother – avoid conflict at all costs.

"I hope you're going to pick up this damn dog. It's not used to being anywhere but Dad's house, and it's driving Dolly crazy. It's breaking things and bleeding all over and I'm sick of the thing."

"Well, hello to you, too," McKenzie mustered the courage to edge a little big-city-steel into her tone.

"Yeah, well. It's been a hell of a week, with Dad keeling over and leaving all of us in a mess. This bee business is unbelievable. I can't understand how he let himself get stung that way. I thought he was smarter than that. Anyway, he was perfectly healthy and all of a sudden he just goes and dies on us and leaves me to deal with everything by myself."

"Well, I'm here now and maybe I can help with the 'mess.'" McKenzie's stress level rose to New York intensity, something she hoped she had left there.

William softened a little, "We've got that damned thing about the will at the attorney's office tomorrow and the funeral and all that to deal with. Dolly's going nuts with the dog here and I just want all of this to be over."

"How about if I pick up the dog and see what I can do with her. That should ease things a little for you. I'm okay with being at the house for now and Otis said there's some dog food here someplace. What's the address again?"

"We're at 100 Spring Blossom Parkway, on the east side of the lake. You already saw Otis?"

"Yes, I saw him briefly yesterday. He hasn't changed a bit and it was good to see him after so long."

"Yeah, well, hurry up and pick up this damned dog and we'll deal with things tomorrow." William promptly hung up.

"Whew. I'm glad that's over," McKenzie sighed with relief and prepared herself for the short trip to William's to pick up

Goldie 2. She braced herself for seeing Dolly. They never did see eye to eye and there was something unnerving about the woman. From the first time they met, Dolly treated McKenzie like a child or someone who was not too bright. She remembered Dolly's comment the first time they spoke, when McKenzie was in high school: "Oh yes, so this is McKenzie, the little sister who likes salamanders better than people."

So where was Sophia, William and Dolly's daughter? She was only two when McKenzie fled after her mother's funeral. She had seen a few pictures through the years but had never spoken with the girl and William hadn't even mentioned her in their brief phone conversation. Oh my gosh, she thought, Sophia would be eighteen years old by now.

Feeling a little rankled, McKenzie decided to put on some makeup and wear one of her New York pantsuits to give her a little more courage. She even put on some heels, 'power shoes' as she thought of them, to give her a height advantage, and then jumped in her rental car.

William, Dolly, and Sophia lived on the other side of the lake in an upscale housing development. Her father had the house built for William and Dolly a few years after her mother died. Huge and beautiful homes were built along the lake shore development with boathouses that held pricey water toys. Meticulous lawns surrounded the mini-mansions, all certainly cared for by "help." Their house seemed to have more flowers than others in the neighborhood and it was beautiful. McKenzie pulled into the driveway and parked next to a new, dark blue BMW sedan.

Standing before the massive front door to an enormous and imposing residence, she rang the bell. Almost before the chimes stopped – it was Beethoven's 5th she noticed with an inward grin – William opened the door in a rush.

He filled the doorway and loomed over her. Always tall, William was no longer the trim figure he once was. Not exactly fat, he just seemed big. His brown hair was shorter than she remembered and was already thinning, and his gray-blue eyes snapped as they always did. He was clean-shaven and had lost the silly mustache he once had. He was still a handsome man, she noted, and presumed he was still charming. Charming, that is, to everyone but her.

"Finally," he said, yanking on a leash as a reticent but beautiful Golden Retriever came around his side. She was wearing a choke chain collar that was obviously too tight and the dog coughed as William pulled on it. Her right front foot was wrapped in a huge towel and she could hardly walk. McKenzie's heart broke as she saw the fine-looking dog's obvious misery.

"Dolly and Sophia are out shopping and I have things to do. At least you can take this beast off our hands," he stated bluntly.

McKenzie decided it was wiser to leave than pursue any more interaction with her frustrated brother. She took the dog's leash and led her slowly to her car. With some boosting help, Goldie was able to climb gingerly into the back seat. McKenzie opened the driver's door, looked back and said to William, "See you at the attorney's office tomorrow." He grunted and shut the front door.

She then pulled out of the driveway and stopped on the street just out of sight of the house. She pulled out her cell phone and called Otis to see if he knew of a vet she could call. This dog was in pain and clearly needed help.

"Hey, Otis."

"Hey, yourself. How was your night?"

"The night was fine. The problem is now. I just picked up gorgeous Goldie 2 from William. There's something wrong with her foot. I can see blood oozing out from the big towel wrapped around it. Can you steer me to a vet fast?"

"My friend Ethan is your man. His vet clinic is on Stillwater Road between the church and the junior high. I'll give him a heads-up that you're on the way."

"Thanks, I'll let you know what happens." McKenzie drove off and glanced at Goldie lying in the back seat and looking at her expectantly. "Poor baby, I wonder what happened to you?"

McKenzie found the vet's clinic easily and wished she had stopped at the house to change her shoes. "It can't be helped," she mumbled and opened the door for Goldie. She had to help the dog get out and walked slowly to the building with Goldie's three-legged gait.

Inside, McKenzie was greeted by a pert dark-haired receptionist with a name tag that said she was Ginny. There was one other woman in the waiting room with a big black cat on her lap. The cat ignored Goldie. A good-looking, brown-haired man came into the room, and said, "Hello there, I'm Ethan Thompson," shaking her hand. "Otis just called me, and it sounds like we've got a problem with our beautiful Goldie." He leaned down to gently pat Goldie's velvety ears, and it was obvious they knew each other as Goldie's tail thumped the floor. Dr. Thompson looked at the woman in the waiting room, "Mrs. Olson, do you mind if I take a closer look at this? I don't like what's happening with this dog's foot, and your Toby's shots could wait a little while if it's okay with you."

The woman nodded and picked up a magazine, with a sideways glance at McKenzie's shoes.

"Let's bring her in here," the doctor said and gently took the leash, leading both of them into the examining room. It smelled slightly of disinfectant, but not unpleasantly, and everything was clean and gleaming.

"So you're McKenzie. I'm sorry about your dad. I knew him well and he was a fine man. Otis said you've just come from New York. Do you know what happened to Goldie?"

"Thank you, Doctor, and no, I don't know what happened. Goldie was at my brother William's house and he said something about something being broken and Goldie bleeding, but that's all I know. Do you know William and Dolly?"

"Yes, I know them. They aren't what I'd call animal lovers," he said bluntly. "I hope you are."

"I haven't had a pet for many years now, but the first Goldie was my all-time love."

"Your dad went without a dog for several years after she died, and finally found this beauty. She was brought to a shelter because she was getting too big for the former owner's house. Actually, I'm responsible for James taking her. I knew he liked Goldens and one day when we were fly fishing together, I told him about a couple of young dogs I had seen when I was at the shelter to give shots to the animals. He went to the shelter and after one lick, I knew he was hooked. Goldie's about three years old now and she's a good dog." He was unwrapping the towel from the dog's foot. "Let's see what's wrong here."

Blood was still oozing, and before McKenzie looked away she could see not one, but several large cuts in the pads on her foot. "Oh boy, Goldie, what have you been into?" Doctor

Thompson muttered as he checked the cuts and bent his head, all attention focused on the dog. He became quiet and gathered the tools he needed for stitching. He turned to McKenzie and said, "You might want to sit over there while I deal with this. It looks worse than I thought." He pointed to a chair in the corner of the room.

Gratefully, she sat. Doctor Thompson gave the dog a shot – for pain, she supposed – and cleaned the wounds. He stitched up the worst cuts and said the rest would heal on their own. At the end, he put on a sort of boot to protect the foot. He also put on one of those big cone collars that look so funny, but keep the dog from biting or licking the boot off. He said she only needed to wear the collar for a few days. He wanted to see her again in a week, and McKenzie began to wonder how long she'd be in town.

After all was finished with the operation and Goldie was lying quietly on the table, he said, "Miss Ward, we need to talk about this more seriously," and he sat down beside McKenzie.

"Call me McKenzie, please. And what do you mean, seriously?"

"Thanks, McKenzie, I'm Ethan. I'm sad to report this dog didn't do this to herself. There is no way she could have stepped on a piece of broken glass and got this many deep cuts in her foot. From the position and depth of the cuts, I believe someone has deliberately harmed this dog."

McKenzie gasped and her eyes widened. "I just picked her up at my brother's house. I've never even seen her before."

"I'm not accusing you, I've already seen how gentle you are with her and I don't think you could have done this. I'm not accusing William or Dolly either, but someone has hurt this dog. I have to report it to the Deputy Sheriff, so I'll be calling

Otis. You can take Goldie home now. She'll be groggy for a while, but keep the cone on her so she doesn't try to get the boot off. Are you staying at your dad's house while you're here?"

"Yes, I am."

"That's good. Goldie will be comfortable there. Your dad always bought food for her from me and there should be a supply at the house. Also, get rid of this choke chain and use the collar and leash that should be at the house, too. I may stop tomorrow to see how she's doing and again, I want to see her here in a week."

"Thank you Doctor, I mean Ethan. I'll take good care of Goldie," McKenzie said with her head full of questions. Ethan then helped her get the sleepy dog to the car.

"Do you think you can get her into the house okay by yourself? I've got to take care of Mrs. Olson's cat or I'd come with you."

Then, Ethan changed his mind. "Actually, it's almost lunchtime, and if you can wait a few minutes while I give the cat a shot, I'll follow you home and help get Goldie into the house. She's a big dog, and you're not exactly dressed for carrying her."

McKenzie decided then and there that her New York clothes – and especially the shoes – would stay in the closet during her remaining time in Deep Lake.

CHAPTER 7
TUESDAY AFTERNOON

McKenzie drove home, grateful that Ethan was following in his car. Pulling up behind her in the driveway, the vet wasted no time joining her to help with Goldie. Using the sling-like canvas bag he'd used at his office to get her to the car in the first place, he transported her into the house, settling her on her comfortable doggie bed in the kitchen.

McKenzie, meanwhile, got the dog a fresh dish of water.

"It's natural that Goldie's still groggy," Ethan explained. "She'll brighten up after a good nap. The water will be extremely helpful, after her blood loss. She'll likely recover in a few days."

"That's a relief."

"I'm going to talk with Otis about what happened to Goldie. I want him to do some checking on William's neighborhood to see if we can find any kids in that area who might have done something like this. I can't imagine any adult deliberately hurting an animal like this."

"Neither can I," McKenzie had a lump in her throat as she watched the kindness with which Ethan handled the dog. She was struck by his gentle and caring manner and couldn't help comparing his actions with how she imagined a New York veterinarian would have handled a similar situation. "I'll watch her this afternoon and is it okay if I call you if anything looks unusual?"

"Yes, call me if anything looks odd," he said, pulling a card out of his pocket. "Here are numbers for my office and home. I'll be home tonight with my daughter, but please call if Goldie doesn't come around or if anything seems not right. I'll stop in the afternoon tomorrow if that works for you."

"That's perfect. I'll see you then. And, thank you for all you've done. Your kindness is most appreciated."

Ethan shook her hand and looked her straight in the eye before he left. He also gently hugged Goldie and ran his hand down the soft fur on her neck to the thick white/golden fur on her chest. Her butt swayed with pleasure. "What a nice man," McKenzie thought. "He's just a plain ordinary nice man."

*****

Concerned about Goldie and still pondering the tender handshake with Ethan and the gentle look in his warmhearted brown eyes, her cell phone jolted McKenzie out of her meditative moment.

It was Michael. She felt a little guilty for not answering his previous call or texts, and she picked up. "Hi Michael, how are things there?"

"Mad, as usual. I've got a new client with too much money and no patience. He wants to sue everybody for everything; just the kind of client I like. How about there? Have you had your father's funeral yet?"

"No. I told you it's on Thursday."

"Oh. So, when are you coming back?"

"I don't know. Things are more complicated than I thought. It could take an extra week to take care of things here. Gayle can handle things in my office. I'm glad I went with Desiree, she's going to be terrific." About six months before her father's death, McKenzie had invited a partner into her commercial real estate business. Desiree Canard, a smooth French bombshell, was already proving to be as competent as she was beautiful.

"Another week! What about the gala for the mayor's latest crusade?"

"I'm sure you'll find someone at the office to fill in. How about Mavis?"

"She's liable to skewer the mayor to the wall. You know how fired up she gets when someone doesn't agree with her politics. At least you're diplomatic."

They both laughed. McKenzie thought about how totally different things were between her New York world and the one she was already rediscovering in Deep Lake. It was like the two were impossible to compare. If she was back in New York right now, she and Michael might be planning to meet at their favorite little bar in Manhattan. He would drink a Belvedere martini while she sipped on a good red wine. They would talk about their days and complain about the people they had to deal with. Maybe they'd see *Kinky Boots* on Broadway again. She loved that show! Afterward, they might get a bite to eat at Joe Allen's, or grab a slice at the great little pizza place over on 9th Avenue, depending on how hungry they were. It would be late. He would aim a kiss at her cheek and they'd head toward their separate apartments ...

She sighed inwardly and said, "Michael, I have a lot to deal with here and at this moment I can't tell you when I'll be back.

I'm sorry to make this short, but I have to run now, so I'll have to talk to you later, okay?"

"Okay." On an impatient gust of breath, Michael hung up, without asking how she was coping, without a kind word, without … or was she the one who cut him off too quickly? Did they always communicate in this curt and abrupt way and she just hadn't noticed?

McKenzie couldn't help thinking about how Michael must look right now, with what was becoming a permanent frown on his face. She admitted to herself he was developing a look of distaste that had lately been there more often than not. Her mind went back to the kindness in Ethan's warm brown eyes. She shook her head and told herself to get real.

Goldie was still snoring and making little whimpers in her sleep, which gave McKenzie a pain in her heart. She went upstairs to change clothes. Relaxed jeans and a loose shirt felt right for now. She may have to rethink going to Otis's for the evening, depending on how Goldie did later.

She tried to do a little work via email with her partner. Her father's no-password Wi-Fi let her connect instantly, but she made a note to fix that down the line. Even small towns needed some degree of security. Desiree was doing great and McKenzie decided to let her take care of what needed to be done. What a good find, to get Desiree on board. She was bright and sharp and could hold her own with the "sharks," as she tended to think of her clients. "Am I getting soft?" McKenzie thought. "I've only been gone two days, and I feel like it's been weeks. Why am I putting off doing work I love?"

McKenzie checked her clothing and shoes and decided she needed to do a little shopping for more appropriate Midwest attire. Where to go? She made a mental note to ask Otis's wife.

She also needed a little hair trim, as she didn't take time for it before leaving the city. Maybe tomorrow after the will reading. "That should be a fun time, not," she said aloud, already dreading the session with William and Dolly.

The afternoon flew by and before long, Goldie was shakily standing in her corner. McKenzie petted and loved her up a little. She then put on her more comfortable collar and leash while the dog lapped at her water dish. She even ate a little food and seemed stronger. The two of them ventured cautiously down the stairs and outside to the back yard. They had already developed a good trust level in their short time together. Goldie hobbled around doing what she needed to do, while McKenzie sat in the garden swing her dad had bought for her mother many years before. After the short outing, McKenzie used a plastic bag – kept at the ready near the dog food, thanks to her dad – to collect Goldie's leavings, and she followed the dog as she slowly climbed the stairs. After another good drink, Goldie collapsed on her pallet, and it looked like she was down for the count.

With perfect timing, the phone rang. It was Otis asking if she thought she could leave Goldie long enough to come for a quick supper with them. He obviously knew the situation after talking with Ethan, and she was eager to talk with him as well as to meet his family. She told him she thought it would be fine to leave the dog alone for a couple of hours.

CHAPTER 8
TUESDAY EVENING

Goldie was out like a light – oboy, McKenzie realized she was already reverting to small-town sayings. She fully expected to be saying things like "uff da," and "you betcha," any minute. She had only been home for two days and already she was talking – and thinking – like she did sixteen years before.

The Jorgensen house was just a block away, so she walked there on what was a fine warm summer evening. She was still wearing her jeans and comfy shirt, and sneakers. Okay, 'sneakers' was the term in New York, but they were called tennis shoes in Deep Lake, she remembered.

Otis answered her knock and welcomed her in with a big hug. "It's just so good to see you again. You've been gone too long, that's all there is to it. Here is my beautiful and amazing Mary Jo, who puts up with my shenanigans and still pretends to love me. I'm so happy you can finally meet."

McKenzie put out her hand but felt a little awkward. Mary Jo, with light brown curly hair and dimples, and a couple of inches shorter than McKenzie's five-foot-eight, defused the moment by pulling McKenzie into a warm hug. She said, "I've heard so much about you through the years, I feel like you're my best friend, too, McKenzie Ward. Welcome to our home." McKenzie hugged her back and immediately knew she had another true friend in Deep Lake.

Behind Otis were two small versions of himself, tow-headed and adorable. They looked about six and eight, maybe, but McKenzie hadn't been around children for so long, she was at a loss. She looked at them seriously, and said, "Hello, I'm McKenzie, and you are?"

The taller one stood a little straighter, put out his hand to shake hers, and said, "I'm Albert, and I'm eight and three-quarters years old. This is Ben. He's only seven, but he's tough."

McKenzie solemnly shook hands with both of them, and said, "I'm very happy to meet you both, boys. I expect you go to school at Deep Lake Elementary? Your dad and I went there a long time ago."

"Yes," said Albert, "I'm going into fourth grade this fall, and Ben will be in second. Mom went there, too, but she's much younger than Dad. She had Mr. Cole for fourth grade. That's who my teacher will be this year, too. He's cool."

"That's great Albert, I think Mr. Cole came after your dad and I were in junior high, so we didn't get to have him as a teacher. I remember hearing that he was good, though. It sounds like you're lucky."

Mary Jo broke in to say it was time to move into the living room where there was apple juice for the boys and wine for the grownups. As they all relaxed McKenzie asked Mary Jo where she could get some casual clothes. "There are several good places in Maplewood Mall, and there are some good coffee places, too, if you need a break."

"Maplewood Mall – how well I remember," McKenzie laughed. "That's the first place I drove to the day I got my driver's license."

"You weren't alone – I did the same thing, and so did my friends," Mary Jo replied with a giggle. "Of course, after that we discovered the Mall of America and the world changed again."

The evening got better and better and McKenzie fell completely in love with Albert and Ben. They were a little shy but respectful and curious, and listened and contributed to exchanges throughout the evening. Mary Jo had made a delicious roast chicken dinner with mashed potatoes and gravy, and vegetables from her own garden. The chicken had come from a farm outside town and tasted better than the most expensive restaurant in NYC. McKenzie was full to bursting when Mary Jo brought in a raspberry pie, made with early berries the boys had picked only days before. It was topped with ice cream and a tiny splash of raspberry liqueur that Mary Jo and Otis had made.

"If I eat one more bite, I'll explode," McKenzie announced, "and wouldn't that be a terrible mess?"

The boys giggled and grinned, but they all ate the pie and were glad of it. It was by far the best meal McKenzie could remember since her mother's meals so long ago. McKenzie was seeing a myriad of reasons why Mary Jo and Otis were perfect together, and she was so happy for her old friend.

"I'm sorry to eat and run, but I have to get home to check on Goldie."

"Dad told us she got hurt, and that's sad. She's a great dog. We've got a dog, too, but she's outside in the kennel 'cuz we've got company," Ben offered. "Her name is Honey, and she is Goldie's sister."

"She is? Why I didn't know that. I'd love to meet Honey, but it will have to be another day. Maybe you could bring her to visit Goldie and we could all have a treat if that's okay with your mom."

Mary Jo interjected, "Of course it's okay, and the boys would love it. We'll be talking to find the right time."

Leave-taking was a typical Minnesota goodbye, with numerous hugs, smiles, and thank-yous all around. "It's like finally meeting a legend," Mary Jo teased McKenzie. "You are entangled in so many of Otis's childhood tales."

"Some tall tales, if I know Otis."

Otis put a hand on his heart. "Hey, I always speak the truth and nothing but."

"We did have a great time as kids," McKenzie conceded. "I can't imagine a better friend then or now."

Otis kissed his wife with casual affection. "Okay if I walk Kenzie home?"

"Sure. Just don't come home with a salamander in your pocket!"

McKenzie knew Otis had been wanting to talk with her after speaking with Ethan. "Otis, this night is one I will treasure forever. Your family is beyond wonderful and I can see how perfect Mary Jo is for you. And those boys! I didn't want to let them go and was afraid I'd embarrass them. They brought back so many memories of when we were their age. I can see why you are such a happy man."

"Yes, they are great, all of them. I don't know what I did to hit the jackpot with Mary Jo, but she puts up with me and I will be forever grateful. I'm sure she'll be calling you to help you get settled in with the dog for the week. You know our number, so let either of us know if you need anything."

He continued, "I need to talk a little about Goldie. Ethan was upset when he called me today. He believes someone deliberately cut the dog's foot. I can't believe that William or Dolly would do such a thing, but I did talk with them about it. They were shocked and thought she had cut herself on broken glass from something she swept off the table with her tail. They said they didn't notice she was bleeding so badly until later. I've started talking with some of the teenagers in that area and their parents. There are a couple of older boys who have been pulling some pranks – dropping firecrackers down the book return slot at the library and that sort of thing. They deny hurting the dog but I'm still working on it. Is Goldie okay?"

"Yes, she's doing much better. Ethan is stopping to check on her later tomorrow, and I think she'll be okay. He did a good job of sewing her up."

"Here we are already. Well, please call me if anything else strange happens. Ethan's a good man and I trust his judgment on what might have happened with the dog. Ethan was a good friend to your dad; they liked to fly fish together sometimes and I know he will miss James. Ethan's wife died a few years ago – cancer – and he's got a little girl about five or so. He just lives a few blocks away, down on Spruce, near my folk's house.

Thanks for coming tonight. It might have helped get your mind off things and I know Mary Jo and the kids loved meeting you. Good luck tomorrow. Your dad was a smart man and I know he will have done what's right with his will. You gonna be okay?"

"Of course I will. I loved meeting your family, and I look forward to seeing them again. I'll be fine tomorrow – and the next day. I just have to do this one day at a time. We'll be talking, and thanks for being there for me. You're still the best friend I ever had."

"G'night Kenzie, that friend thing works both ways, you know." Otis turned for home.

Goldie hadn't budged since McKenzie left and she was still sound asleep. McKenzie gave her a gentle pat on her soft head and went upstairs for the night.

CHAPTER 9
THE WILL

McKenzie woke early after the best night's sleep she'd had in a long time. Goldie was sitting up and stretching. She gave a big yawn and positively grinned at McKenzie with her tail wagging her whole backside. Together, they went outside and stumbled down the steps. McKenzie had grabbed her cell phone that had been left plugged in in the kitchen overnight. She sat on the step and checked it while Goldie limped around the yard and did her business.

There were several texts from Michael, and he was not happy. "Where R U?" and "Call me" were the latest.

With a sigh, she called him, expecting he was still at home even though it was an hour later there.

Michael picked up, "So where have you been? I tried all night and you never answered. What's going on there?"

So much for "Good morning, it's good to hear from you," McKenzie thought.

"I was busy here – we had some trouble with the dog, and…"

Michael interrupted, "What dog? You have to deal with a dog there, too?"

"She's really a sweetheart and she was good company for my dad for the past few years. I'll handle it. How are you doing?"

"Got a meeting with my new client in thirty minutes. Things are tolerable."

"I have a meeting with Dad's attorney to go over his will this morning, and some other things to do so it's going to be a busy day for me. I'd better let you go so you can get to your meeting."

"Already on the way. Talk to ya later." Michael hung up abruptly and McKenzie looked at the phone. She hadn't thought about it before but now she wondered about her own conversations. Could she be coming across too sharply when dealing with others as Michael just did with her? Kindness isn't reserved for Minnesota, she reminded herself.

Goldie was ready to go in the house and it was time to think about the meeting. The cone on Goldie's head was getting in the way some but McKenzie settled her with food and water and Goldie looked like a nap was already on the way when McKenzie headed upstairs to get ready.

The Armani suit would work for the day, and McKenzie slipped on some flats rather than the power shoes. She applied minimal makeup and said to her reflection in the mirror, "Well, here I go, Dad, I wonder what surprises are in store for me today?" Goldie was sleeping soundly as she went out to her car and headed for the attorney's office on Main Street.

*****

McKenzie arrived at Dave Manson's office about the same time as William, Dolly, and Sophia. Ed Johnson was also coming up the steps, and McKenzie wondered why he was to be at the will reading. He gave her a nod and a small smile.

"Good to see you McKenzie, but I'm sorry it has to be this way. Are you staying in town a while?"

"Only for a few days, Ed. It's good to see you, too."

Dolly drew McKenzie into her arms in a sisterly embrace that felt false. "It's good to see you after so long, but what a sad day it is, isn't that right?"

"Yes, it is a sad day," McKenzie mumbled against Dolly's ample bosom because Dolly was standing on a step above her. "Hello Will," she said as she escaped Dolly's hug.

"Yeah," William said. "I wonder what surprises Dad has in store for us today," looking at Ed Johnson.

Ed, a pleasant-looking man about sixty or so, was wearing a suit for the occasion. He seemed to be a little embarrassed to be there, but he shook hands with William and gave his condolences to McKenzie and Dolly.

McKenzie was a little surprised that Sophia was now a virtual picture of her mother, small and blond, and very pretty with a well-shaped nose and nice-looking mouth. Sophia said quietly, "Hi Aunt McKenzie," which immediately made her feel old.

Dave Manson, a small man in his mid-sixties and perfectly groomed, greeted the group and ushered all of them into his conference room. "I hated to see this day come, and even though I knew James was getting up in age, I thought he was in better health. I expected to have him around for a long time yet. This bee sting business was a terrible surprise and a tragic one for sure. I know the whole town will miss this great man a lot. He did so much for our community as a judge, and after he retired. It is truly a sad day."

All of them agreed and nodded at Manson as he continued.

"We are here to talk about James's will. He made some recent changes in his will and you may be surprised at some of what's in it. James was in good health, as I've said, and his mind was clear and sound to the end. What you are going to hear is what he wanted to be done with his money and possessions, and I hope you will honor his wishes."

Everyone looked around the room but avoided each other's eyes.

Manson began to read the details of the will. There were a number of bequests for charities and specific local organizations, including their church, the fire department, and others. He read through the rather lengthy list and McKenzie was pleased with her father's attention to his community. He really was a good man, and she began to feel pangs of guilt for not seeing him for such a long time.

Manson then looked at McKenzie and said, "McKenzie, James has given you the family house and all of its contents, plus his car. You are to deal with your father's possessions as you see appropriate. He specifically asks that you take care of his dog if it survives him, and it appears the dog has survived. I have to insert here that James notes he has already built a new house for William and his family which is worth significantly more than the old family home." Dolly gave a small satisfied-looking smile at this revelation.

Manson continued, "There are funds of a sizeable amount left to the family, but James chose to have a trust fund set up with money distributed over the next twenty years evenly split between the two of you, McKenzie and William. I will give each of you a statement for the amount of the payments at a later date. He specifically wanted the distribution done this way because both of you have what he considered adequate income for daily living, and he wanted the money preserved for later in your lives.

"Additional funds are in trust for Sophia, James's only grandchild at this point, and distribution will start when she reaches the age of twenty-five. This is in addition to college funds which are not touchable by anyone except the college Sophia chooses to attend."

Sophia and Dolly exchanged puzzled looks.

"We come now to the trucking company, Ward Transport. Ed Johnson has competently managed the company since James's father's death. It is comfortably in the black, with a number of company drivers and owner/operators as well. Ed, James appreciated what you have done with the company over the years. He wants you to continue to be at the helm of the company for the foreseeable future." He referred to the wording of the will, "Ownership of the company has been placed in a trust and Ed Johnson is to serve as president and chief operations manager until his retirement or death."

Dolly gave a sudden gasp and her hand flew to her mouth. With widened eyes, she blurted, "But what about ..."

Dave Manson cut her off, reading again directly from the will, "After Ed Johnson's retirement or death, ownership of the company will pass to William and McKenzie equally. Until that time, William has a lifetime job doing what he has been doing for the past number of years," Manson paused, looked at William and said, "as long as his performance reviews warrant continuation of his position. These performance reviews will be completed by the president, Ed Johnson."

Dolly jumped to her feet, "Well I never! This is outrageous! How could he treat his son this way?"

William was glowering but didn't say anything, and Ed Johnson looked more embarrassed than ever.

Manson said, "This completes the reading of the will of James Archer Ward. Of course, any of you have the right to contest the will. But, as I said before, William was in complete control of his senses and I consider this will to be an accurate portrayal of his wishes. I would seriously discourage any of you to think about contesting it."

William stood, grabbed Dolly with one hand and Sophia with the other, and said, "Let's get out of here." Without another word, they stomped out of the room.

McKenzie and Johnson looked at Dave Manson with questions on their faces. Manson said, "Well, that went as I expected. I hope you're okay with James's wishes."

McKenzie stood, "Thank you, Dave. I know my father respected you, and it appears that he knew his family well. Ed, I can only thank you for taking care of Ward Transport as well as you have done through the years. However, I'm afraid your job just got tougher. Do you know why Dad set things up this way?"

Johnson replied, "Yes, James knew his son. William likes to have an office where he can hang out away from home if you get my meaning. He draws a generous salary. He does make some sales once in a while, but I'm afraid it's not his favorite thing to do, and I can't depend on him to be consistent. Golf and other sports are much more important to William, to be honest. I love the company and I think your dad made the right decision about it, but William is not going to take this well."

Johnson continued, "Thank you, Dave. You did a good job today of expressing James's wishes and I know it wasn't easy for you. McKenzie, I'm so glad to see you back here in Deep Lake. We've missed you. Now you've got a house to take care of – not to mention a dog. You may have some big decisions to make in your life. I hope you choose well. You're welcome to stop by the company any time to see how things are going. I'll see you tomorrow, of course, and I hope to see you again soon." Johnson shook hands with both of them and left the room.

McKenzie sighed, "Well, that's over. Now it seems that we all have to live with the consequences. Thank you again, Dave. I'm sure we'll be in touch. See you tomorrow?"

"Of course, I'm a pallbearer for your dad. He had everything pre-arranged, so I'm sure the funeral will go like clockwork. I'm sorry about William and Dolly, but I sort of expected that kind of reaction. William doesn't hold his temper well, and Dolly, well Dolly is just Dolly, I guess."

"I'll see you tomorrow," and McKenzie walked down the steps with mixed feelings of relief and bewilderment.

*****

McKenzie's mind was filled with confusion as she got into her car. It wasn't even noon and it seemed like her whole world had changed or morphed into something she couldn't get her thoughts around. She needed to sort it all out and it wasn't going to happen quickly.

Instead of driving, she sat in the car and sort of decompressed after the will reading event.

She began to look around and noted that the town hadn't changed a bit. She remembered the old men who used to sit in front of the barbershop every morning. She stole a glance, and unbelievably, they were still there – well, this was likely a new generation of them, but sitting on a bench in front of the barbershop across the street were three elderly men. As she remembered from years ago, they always wore summer caps covering balding heads, and baggy, bland and colorless pants and shirts. They didn't talk much, but there was a laugh now and then about something or someone. McKenzie knew the group must change through the years, but somehow, they were always there, and they always looked the same. She couldn't help wondering who would be sitting there when she was their age.

Next to the barbershop was the local beauty shop. "Sassy Janice's House of Hair," the sign said. "Janice," McKenzie thought, "could it possibly be my Janice?" In high school, McKenzie was friends with Janice Hopkins, the daughter of Deep Lake's only black family at the time. Her dad worked for Ward Transport and Janice was vivacious and high-spirited. She had come from an inner-city school in Chicago, and Deep Lake was small potatoes to her. She kept herself aloof from other kids, who saw her as cheeky.

The first day of tenth-grade typing class she had sat next to McKenzie. They ignored each other at first. Then one day at lunch the tables were full and they accidentally sat down next to each other. Janice made a rude comment about McKenzie's unruly blond hair which hadn't yet settled into something she could manage. Janice said, "You'd be better off if you just cut it all off and start over."

"Oh yeah?" McKenzie replied, "Who's gonna cut it, you?"

Janice backed off, but the exchange started them talking. Later in typing class, they continued to fling comments at each other. Before long, the two of them began an insolent and mischievous competition with typing that lasted through the semester and then blossomed into friendship. They had each grown up with different perspectives and experiences and both found it fascinating to learn about how the other had lived. Because they respected each other's attitudes and ideas, they had some terrific deep-seated arguments over lunch that usually ended with appreciation for the other's opinions. McKenzie was basically shy and she admired Janice's smart-alecky attitude of life. She also admired Janice's gorgeous head of inky-black hair which was braided or ponytailed or woven into beautiful creations every day by her mother. Janice's mother eventually did cut off most of McKenzie's hair and styled it simply, so McKenzie could fix it more easily herself.

The girls remained friends throughout high school until McKenzie went away to college, but they lost touch after that.

McKenzie decided on the spot that she needed a little trim and "Sassy Janice's House of Hair" sounded like just the place she needed to go.

She walked across the street to the beauty shop and as she opened the shop door, a chirpy tune announced visitors. As she had hoped, it was Sassy Janice herself with a headful of tiny braids held back by a beautiful butterfly clip, who came to say, "May I help you?"

McKenzie answered with "I can still type faster than you can, but I can't cut hair, can you?"

"Kenzie, you're really here! It's about time, girl, I've been waiting for this day for sixteen years!" Janice yelled loud enough to jolt everyone in the shop. "Let me look at you, you skinny thing. Who's been hacking your hair in that big city? I think you need some of Janice's sassy scissors."

By that time the two of them were hugging and dancing and kissing each other's cheeks, and the whole shop was wondering what was going on.

"I knew you'd do it someday, when did you get your own place? And how did it all come about? Oh, we have so much catching up to do!" McKenzie was ecstatic for her old friend and couldn't stop grinning.

As she began to look around the shop, she did a double-take and saw one of the other stylists in the shop was none other than Vidal Vargas. He was another one from their class, who was most definitely a guy when they were in high school. He had been an exchange student from South America and obviously came back to stay, but somehow along the line, he changed his gender. He was a flashy dresser then and still appeared to be, with skin-tight wildly printed yoga pants, platform heels, and a flowing eye-popping top.

"Hey Vidal – good to see that you're working with Janice. How have you been?"

"I'm great, and it's good to see you, too. I'm Vicky now, and I love working with Janice. We're all sorry about your dad, but I guess that's what it took to get you back to Deep Lake, huh?"

"Well, yes, that's why I'm here. It's been a little rough, but I'll get it all sorted out. The funeral's tomorrow."

"Of course it is, sweetie," said Janice. "We've been working overtime getting the mayor's wife dolled up and all the church elders' wives, too, not to mention all the other ladies in town who admired your dad. This place has been jumpin'. Even so, I've always got time to take care of you. Want a little trim?" she said while plopping McKenzie in a chair and whipping out a fresh cape and towel.

"Oboy, this is exactly what I need, Janice. Now just remember, don't do it like you did in tenth grade, and turn my hair green, right?" The two of them reverted immediately to giggling teenagers and reveled in each other's company.

Two hours flew by with a wash and a trim and much chatter all around. Vicky even sneaked in a quick manicure all the while complaining about the sorry state of McKenzie's nails and the incompetence of all New York City's manicurists. Suddenly, McKenzie remembered that Ethan Thompson was coming to check on Goldie and she had to get home.

"Ethan Thompson?" squealed Janice. "You're in town for two days and you've already got a date with Ethan Thompson? He's the hottest thing in town and he hasn't got time for anybody. Poor guy lost his wife and he just buried himself in work. He finally brought that little girl of his in for a haircut when she got to looking like a homeless waif. He never got the hang of doing her hair. We fixed her up and now he brings her in regular. How'd you get hooked up with him?"

"It's not a date, he's taking care of my dad's dog. Goldie got hurt and he sewed her up yesterday and he's just coming over to check on her, that's all."

"Hmmmm. House calls for the dog. Now I've heard everything," Janice chuckled. "Well, you just get on home and don't be late for Dr. Thompson. It's great to have you back, Kenzie. No matter how long it's been, you haven't changed a bit. There's a new sports bar in town that serves some pretty good local brews plus some new cocktails that'll knock your socks off. We can get down to the really good stuff about the past sixteen years there."

"Thanks, Janice, and Vicky, too. This has been the best part of coming back to Deep Lake. I'll see you tomorrow." McKenzie flew out the door and headed home.

*****

Back at the house, Goldie was stirring and stretching. She looked a little stronger than the night before and after a good drink of water for both of them, McKenzie took the dog out the back door. Sitting in the garden swing felt so natural by now, and she thought over the morning as Goldie sniffed around the yard.

William and Dolly were definitely not happy with the results of the will reading, and McKenzie realized that things couldn't be good with William's job, the way the will was worded. Poor Ed Johnson. He had his work cut out for him now more than ever, she feared. She wondered about Sophia and what her plans were for college. She was a pretty girl, looked just like her mother, in fact, and McKenzie would like to get to know her better. She wasn't sure how to do that, considering William's gruffness and Dolly's outright hostility after that morning. What a dilemma.

Lost in her thoughts, she looked up suddenly and saw Ethan Thompson coming into the yard. He was wearing a "professional veterinarian" look. He wore dark pants and a striped dress shirt, with casual boots and his kind smile. Goldie had finished her sniffing and was lying comfortably next to the swing.

"Isn't this a cozy sight," Ethan said, "looks like the two of you are getting along okay."

"Oh, hi Ethan. Yes, Goldie is a sweetheart. She's doing better already and it doesn't look like she's trying to get the boot off at all."

"That's good. I think we'll leave the cone on for another day just to be sure. I'm going to change the bandage now and maybe we'll take the cone off tomorrow after the funeral. Work for you?"

"Whatever you say – you're the doc."

Ethan leaned down and started unwrapping Goldie's foot. He had a gentle touch and Goldie didn't mind at all. She seemed to know he was making her better. McKenzie was impressed. They kept up a light banter about the town and soon the foot was bandaged up again and Ethan said the wounds looked much better.

"May I sit with you a minute?" he asked, and at her nod, he joined her in the swing. "I've talked with Otis about what might have happened to Goldie and we can't get anywhere. It might have been the kids I was talking about who did this, but they say they didn't do it. I'm afraid we'll never know exactly what happened, but I'm sure going to keep watching for anything else like this. This was a cruel act on the part of someone."

"I agree. I'm sorry you can't find out what happened, but I can take care of her for now and you can trust that I'll keep watch out for her."

"How long are you planning to be in Deep Lake?"

"I'm not really sure. I had expected to be here only a week or so, but things are getting a little more complicated and it could be longer. Dad left me the house and I understand there's a car in the garage – I haven't even looked yet. And there's Goldie ... I have a business in New York, but I'm lucky to have some competent people there who can take care of it for a while. How's that for a vague answer," she laughed.

"Life gets complicated for everybody, I guess. We're all a little vague at times. Well, I'd better be on my way. I'm one of the pallbearers for tomorrow, so I'll see you then. There's a lunch in the church basement planned for after the service and burial, and I expect there will be a pretty big crowd. Your dad was very well-liked in our town. Are you up for all of that?"

"It's all coming back to me – I remember the church ladies working in the kitchen for funerals and Mom always had to take bars for those events at Hope Lutheran. Hope – what a nice name. Never thought about it till now, but it sounds good to me. Now I'm getting nostalgic," she laughed again.

"I've gotta run – you'll do fine tomorrow, I can tell Deep Lake's getting back into your blood. When the whole funeral and the aftermath are over, I'll stop here later in the afternoon and look at Goldie again if that works for you."

"I'd appreciate it. Thank you so much for coming. You're a kind man and I appreciate your being a friend to my dad. I can see already why he liked you."

"It was my good luck to have such a friend. We've both lost a good man. See ya tomorrow," Ethan said as he walked away.

"Well Goldie, looks like it's you and me tonight. It's time I took a better look around my new house." McKenzie led Goldie into the house to her comfortable corner bed and then went to check out the garage. Inside was a fairly new SUV. McKenzie didn't know much about cars, but this looked both comfortable and like it could handle the rough roads in the country where her dad liked to fish and hunt. "Nice car, Dad, thanks," she said softly.

Back in the house, she discovered several plates of cookies and bars in the kitchen that may have been brought by thoughtful neighbors. Somebody must have let them in – or they knew about the key above the back door, most likely. Her presence had been noted by the neighborhood, obviously. Even though the house was locked, in the refrigerator were a couple of casseroles that looked delicious. She fed Goldie and heated up a plate from one of the dishes. This caused her to dive back into time when she ate her mother's hotdishes as they called them in the Midwest. "I sure could get used to this," she meditated. In New York, nobody talked to their apartment neighbors beyond a stolen glance when sharing an elevator and a cautious 'good morning' occasionally.

After dinner, she finally remembered to check her phone and there were again several texts from Michael. Guiltily, she called him. "Hey, sorry but I got really busy today and didn't get back to you. How was your day?"

Michael sounded frustrated and a little angry. "I wondered what you were up to. I've had a heavy day and am just headed over to the club for a drink. You should be with me. When are you coming back?"

"Well, that's what I wanted to talk about. Things are a little more complicated here than I thought. We had the will reading today and tomorrow is the funeral and all. I could be here longer than I expected."

"You need to be here where your job is – and me!"

"I know, but it's not that easy. Dad left me the house, and a car, and a dog, and…"

Michael broke in, "So why can't your brother take care of all that? He lives there, doesn't he?"

"As I said, it's not that easy. Michael, I don't want to talk about all this now. I'll call you after the funeral tomorrow and maybe I'll know more about how I can work things out. Is that okay?"

"It'll have to be. G'night," and he hung up.

"What's happening to my nice organized life? And more, why am I getting so comfortable back here in Deep Lake?" McKenzie asked herself as she snuggled her feet under a soft warm dog who sighed at her touch. "I have a lot of sorting out to do, but like Scarlett O'Hara said, 'tomorrow's another day,'" and she headed up to bed.

CHAPTER 10

THE FUNERAL

Thursday dawned with a glowing sunrise on what looked to be a gorgeous – if sad – July day. McKenzie felt the need for a good run so she donned light sweats, did her stretches and took off around the neighborhood. It felt good to run alone without crowds around her, unlike Central Park. Here, there were few even up yet, and nobody got in her way. She got in a good two-mile run around the town where she encountered few people or cars. It gave her strength to deal with the anticipated diversity in emotions she was likely to encounter that day.

McKenzie needed to be at the church early, so she took care of Goldie and got her ready for her after-breakfast nap. Knowing she needed some energy for the day, she sneaked a bite of somebody's delicious chicken hotdish from the fridge, along with her coffee which she enjoyed on the garden swing, and that was enough for breakfast.

She brought out the Armani suit again, this time with a skirt and a light blue shirt. She found some mid-heel shoes that would do, too. There would be a lot of standing that day. Her hair looked great after Janice's trim. She was lucky to inherit her mom's gentle blond waves that, after she grew up, never took much effort to look decent. Thinking back now, Janice's mom had helped with that, too, remembering the first drastic haircut she had given her.

Otis called to make sure she was ready for the onslaught and said he would pick her up so she didn't have to drive to the church. Mary Jo and the boys would come later. One more pat for Goldie who looked at her with adoring eyes, and she headed out the door, leaving the dog settled on her cushy bed in the kitchen.

Otis looked handsome in his dark suit as he opened the car door for her. Looks had never registered with her while they were growing up, and Otis had always been just Otis because their friendship wasn't based on looks. Now, she noticed he had matured into an especially good-looking man. "Ready for the crowd? I'm expecting Hope Lutheran will be bursting at the seams today."

"I think so – this will be an extraordinary day. I haven't seen my cousins or my uncle for all this time either, and I hope I remember more of the people from the town. Memories have been pouring into my mind over the past few days like water into a bowl, and I'm almost at capacity now. I'm afraid I'll be on overflow for the rest of the day."

"You'll be fine, I have no doubt. And Mary Jo and I will be there to hold you up if we need to," and they headed off to the church.

Hope Lutheran Church had all of its doors open to welcome the beautiful morning, and McKenzie remembered their Sunday trips to church. She spent two years in confirmation class, also, and that was okay because her friends were there, too.

The pastor was new to her. He was a young, nice-looking man. Dark-haired and average height with glasses which she suspected he wore because they made him look older. His wife and little boy were close behind. "Hello, McKenzie, Erik

Osterholt. I'm glad to meet you, but I'm sorry it has to be this way. Your dad was a remarkable man. His death was a terrible shock, and we will all miss him."

"Yes, Pastor, it was a shock to me, too, and I'm finding it hard to think about him being gone," she replied, while her mind roiled, *How can this be – not my strong Daddy?*

"Today will be heavy for you and I know you're going to be overwhelmed by the sheer numbers of people. I hope you know that I'll be here for you later when you might need someone to talk with. How about if I stop over on Sunday afternoon to see how you're doing? I know the house, of course. You're welcome to come to services on Sunday, but in any event, I'll stop by your house about two o'clock. Would that work?" McKenzie liked his direct approach, young or not, and his offer was kind. Sunday was three days away and she had no idea what she'd be doing that afternoon. She had been planning to return to New York on Sunday, but she understood more and more that was not going to happen.

"Sounds good, Pastor. Thanks," McKenzie said automatically. He continued to show her where she and the rest of the family were to be and how the service would proceed. William and Dolly had also arrived and drifted around her but didn't speak. Dolly was wearing a beautiful suit in a light taupe color and shoes which looked like they should hurt. People were beginning to arrive and already the church was filling up. It was a good thing it was a nice day because it was already apparent the church steps and grounds would be used as visiting places for small groups to talk together.

The day passed in a blur for McKenzie. William and Dolly were formally holding court near James's urn, greeting guests. The urn itself was made of wood and a picture of James had been burned into the lid. A handsomely framed photo of him was next to the urn along with a masculine-looking floral arrangement.

There were some picture boards that Dolly must have thrown together and they included many shots of their small family and a few of James and Rose. McKenzie saw only one of herself with her parents, but at least there was one, so she had to give Dolly credit. Sophia was in a corner giggling nervously with her girlfriends. It was apparent that none of them knew what to do at this sort of event. Dressed alike in short skirts and dressy tops, they clumped together and seemed to be attached at the shoulder as they moved around the room wondering whether to sit or stand, to smile or not. "Poor kids," McKenzie thought, "they must feel like they're in a foreign country."

Otis was true to his word and he trailed along with McKenzie as she wandered through the room and recognized or was recognized by many individuals. Her Uncle Archie, James's grizzled older brother, had arrived along with his sons and their families. Archie and his wife lived on their farm outside of town, but all of the land had been leased to bigger farms. Archie's son John had one of those huge corporate farms and the other son worked for 3M at their massive headquarters on Highway 94, east of St. Paul, she learned.

Cousin John said, "Well McKenzie, are you thinking of coming back to Deep Lake for good now? I hear your dad left you the house."

News traveled fast, McKenzie thought with a blink. "I'm not ready to consider that yet, John," and she wandered away, slightly rocked by the thought.

The funeral itself was quite formal, but there was caring laughter as Pastor Erik remembered James's kindnesses and generosity with the community. A choir sang and there were hymns. McKenzie was surprised to hear Dave Manson speak a few words, and more surprised when Ethan Thompson gave a short eulogy as well. He really did know her father, she saw, and his kind and humorous fishing story was well received. No one mentioned the wasps.

The burial was quickly done and the worst part of the ordeal was when her father's wooden urn was placed in a small hole next to McKenzie's mother's grave at Hope Cemetery. There was already a headstone for the two of them and her father's death date had only to be added to the stone. This spoke to her father's foresight, but even more, it spoke to the finality of it all to McKenzie. Her tears finally started to fall as Pastor Erik said the final words and Otis on one side and Mary Jo on the other, physically had to hold her upright as they turned away from the grave.

Back at the church, there was a full lunch assembled by the church ladies, and the basement was filled with conversation and stories. William and Dolly made their way around the room acknowledging others and Sophia was still connected to her friends in their mutual discomfort.

McKenzie couldn't eat anything but had an ever-full coffee cup in hand. Janice and Vicky were there to support her and Mary Jo kept a close eye on her, too, while trying to keep her boys from eating all the fudge bars. Otis came and went and at last, the day was waning and most of the guests had gone. William and Dolly had been near her for most of the day, but they hadn't exchanged a single word. Dolly spoke with the church ladies about left-over food being taken to a nearby shelter, and everything else was taken care of by the funeral home including taking flowers to local nursing homes and leaving one large arrangement at the church.

Emotions and memories were neatly wrapped up and put away like the food, and before long, Otis was by her side asking if she was ready to go home. She nodded and in doing so, realized there was nothing more there for her and "home" was where she needed to be.

Strong and steady Otis delivered her to her door. "Ethan said he was stopping over soon to check on Goldie, and Mary Jo and I are coming over later with the boys for supper. Your refrigerator is bursting with hotdishes, so we'll figure something out. It doesn't look like William and Dolly are coming and they may have something going on at their house with people there after the funeral. Does all this work for you?"

McKenzie sighed with gratitude for the kindnesses shown her that day. She gave him a tight hug and a huge thank you for all he and his family had done, and sent him on his way.

In the kitchen after Otis left, she cried into Goldie's soft and willing neck, and hugged her with all her might. "Oh Goldie, what really happened to my dad? Were you there with him? Maybe … oh why, why, why?" she wept until sobs began.

*****

Ethan Thompson came by a while after she had calmed. He checked Goldie out carefully and removed the cone from her neck. "These wounds are healing nicely. Goldie's a healthy dog and I can see she's getting lots of good attention from you, McKenzie." Leaning down to remove the cone, he said to Goldie, "Let's get rid of this pesky cone, eh girl?"

He straightened after rubbing Goldie's neck and said, "I don't think she'll bother the wounds much, and if she licks them, that's all to the good at this point."

McKenzie offered, "The day is still so lovely, let's go outside so Goldie can move around a little now that she's got that awful cone off. "May I get you some lemonade?"

His face brightened. "That would be great."

Ethan and Goldie went out into the yard and when McKenzie came out with two glasses of chilled lemonade, Ethan was already settled on the garden swing. She handed him a glass and sat beside him. She barely knew this man yet felt extremely comfortable in the moment. Words weren't necessary as they watched Goldie gingerly prance around the yard. The tangy drink proved just the thing to soothe her throat. She felt parched from all the chatting she'd done at the funeral and the tears she'd shed.

"She's a beautiful dog," she said wistfully. "Sweet-tempered, joyful."

"That she is. Your dad loved her."

Her throat tightened a little. "Wish I'd seen them together. Wish … I'd come back sooner."

"Don't dwell on that, McKenzie," he said gently. "I doubt he ever questioned your love for him. Sometimes life gets in the way. Sometimes, it seems like there's all the time in the world…"

"Whenever work got in the way, I rationalized a month or two wouldn't matter. That I'd get to Deep Lake in due time. I didn't see the end coming for Dad, especially not a quick and cruel one because of bee stings." Her eyes dampened all over again. "It wasn't like him to be careless with his bee allergy. He carried an EPI-pen with him all the time."

Ethan was frank and honest. "Otis and I have been talking a lot about this, and you need to know what we're looking at. The whole episode just doesn't seem to make sense. James was careful and yes, he did have his EPI-pen with him in the car. However, it appears that he was overwhelmed by a swarm of large wasps. He had so many stings so quickly, that he couldn't get to the medicine that was in the middle console of the car. He was behind the vehicle with the hatchback up when he was attacked."

"Was Goldie with him?"

"Yes, Goldie was with him but we're not sure where she was at the time of the stings. She didn't seem to have any stings on her. He always took her along fishing and she loved to explore the shorelines for anything that moved. It was her chance to run free and she usually took off the moment he opened the car door. We're presuming Goldie came to James after the attack. She was lying beside him when he was found. In fact, they had a hard time taking him away after it was all over, and the ambulance came. She wasn't letting him go willingly.

"I've been waiting to talk about this, but you need to know, and maybe now is the time. Otis called me after they found your dad because he wanted to know more about the behaviors of bees and wasps. We looked everywhere we could think of by that area of the lake and couldn't find a wasp nest anywhere. It is still a total mystery as to where those wasps came from. There should have been a nest in a tree or a fallen log, or somewhere, and we just couldn't find it. We found some little ground wasps at least a hundred yards away, but I don't think it was them. Ground wasps are nasty and they sting multiple times, like other wasps. Bees, on the other hand, only sting once and when they lose their stinger, they die. These stings were from a larger insect, like a paper wasp. Where they came from I have absolutely no idea."

"Do you mean my father's death is still under investigation?"

"Well, I think sort of, unofficially, yes. Otis may know more and I'm sure he means to speak with you when the time is right. I'm so sorry to dump this on you, but I just thought it needed to be said. I loved your dad, too, and I feel so awful about his death. I wish I knew what I could do to help."

"This puts a new light on things. I was planning to go back to New York on Sunday, but I don't see how I can go now. There is just too much up in the air."

"I was hoping you would see things like that. I believe you're where you need to be, McKenzie. Otis told me that he and Mary Jo are coming over tonight to be with you. You'll probably have enough to keep you busy tomorrow, but my clinic is only open until noon on Saturday. How about if I come over again then to see how things are going for you and Goldie. I may have my little girl with me, so I hope that's okay. I like to spend as much time as I can with her on weekends. Maybe we could go out for a pizza or something later."

"That's perfect. You've been so kind and thoughtful through all of this. I'd love to meet your daughter."

As he was leaving shortly after their conversation, they walked toward his car. Ethan took McKenzie's hands and said, "You're exactly as I hoped you would be, McKenzie Ward. I hope you don't think I'm being too forward if I say this. Your dad told me so much about you and I hope you know how proud he was of you and your accomplishments. Under all the accomplishments, however, I was hoping the real you would be just like the woman you are. We'll get all of this figured out before long, and the cloud of sadness will get brighter. We never forget, and we never "get over" the death of a loved one. It does get easier to handle as time goes on, because good memories eventually overcome the bad, and life does go on. You're going to have some big decisions to make about your life, I'm afraid, and I hope they're the right ones. Meanwhile, thank you for being here."

With that, he kissed her gently on the cheek and was gone.

"Wow," McKenzie whispered aloud as she watched Ethan drive away. She sat again in the yard swing with Goldie lying beside her. Everything Ethan had told her was swirling in her mind and the possibility of foul play of some kind in her father's death was like watching a beautiful curtain being ripped away to reveal a horrifying scene behind.

Otis was due soon and she would take this up with him. She shook her head and put away her terrible thoughts, like covering the scene once more with the beautiful curtain.

Her cell phone had several texts from Michael, and a couple from her office. She bit her tongue and called her partner, Desiree. After giving some bland advice and approving basically everything Desiree had done in her absence, Desiree wasn't upset at all about McKenzie having to stay in Minnesota for the foreseeable future. Michael was another matter.

Losing her nerve to call him, she returned a text saying she was forced to stay at least another week. She then went to the kitchen and started pulling out casseroles and goodies which kind neighbors had brought, after plugging in her phone in a far corner where she couldn't hear the expected pings of incoming texts.

CHAPTER 11
AFTER THE FUNERAL

O tis and Mary Jo, plus their boys, Albert and Ben, came over that evening. They had a great time sampling all the dishes brought by neighbors. Mary Jo took over the serving and with lots of laughter, everybody helped clean up. The boys fawned over Goldie and she wiggled her whole body in joy. To top it off, they all played a rousing game of Monopoly and Albert had more hotels than anyone else at the end. It was exactly the sort of evening McKenzie remembered from her youth and she was filled with nostalgia.

"All right, gang, time to head home," Otis finally announced. "It's bath time for one thing."

"Not yet," Albert protested. "I'm still counting my money."

"And I always put the pieces away," Ben chimed in, already folding the game board in half.

"Kenzie's had a long day," Mary Jo put in firmly. "She needs to rest."

It warmed McKenzie's heart as the boys gave her smiles and trusting looks. "I'll have you back for another round soon. Promise. And I won't let you win next time."

"You didn't let us!"

"No way!"

McKenzie chuckled. "I'm teasing. You won fair and square. But it is getting late."

"Thanks, Kenzie," Mary Jo said, grabbing her sweater from the back of a chair.

"Let me get the leftover desserts I promised you." McKenzie headed for the kitchen, swiftly realizing Otis had tagged along. Glad for a private moment, she whirled on him fast near the gaping refrigerator door. "When were you going to tell me about your suspicions about Dad's death? Why did I have to first hear it from Ethan who's almost a stranger?"

Otis looked at his shoes in a rare moment of discomfort. "Seemed awkward, before the burial. And honestly, I was having trouble finding the words. You just seem so fragile."

"Do I? Well, I'm not! Oh, sorry," she ultimately mumbled. "Don't mean to get so hot about it."

"It's okay. It's the old Kenzie I love and miss. Get mad. Get hot. Let's figure this out."

Her soft brows narrowed. "Tomorrow, Otis."

"Damn straight, tomorrow. And Ethan isn't exactly a typical stranger," he added. "You like the guy and he likes you, I can tell."

She shook her head, feeling heat brand her cheeks. "Nothing is ever that simple."

"Sometimes, it is." On that, Otis sidled out of firing range.

McKenzie finally fell into bed totally exhausted, fleetingly remembering she never did talk to Michael after the funeral. It would simply have to wait.

*****

Waking to the sun on her face Friday morning, McKenzie realized she hadn't even closed the window shades the night before, something unthinkable in New York. Warm and snug and still sleepy, she rested in bed and tried to awaken her thoughts along with her body. Everything felt so good there in her family home – so natural.

Ethan was right, it was time for her to make some decisions about her life.

Hardly finished with her morning run and Goldie chores – she was already thinking that when Goldie's foot healed, it would be fun to take her along on her runs – Otis called to set a time for them to meet that day. They decided on lunch at her house, so they could have privacy. Otis would pick up sandwiches at Joe's because the funeral food was getting stale. There were still some pies and cookies to munch on, and they would be good for days, but the casseroles and softer foods were ready to be tossed.

After the call, she tentatively looked at the texts from Michael. At first he was angry at her non-response, but eventual texts showed he was hurt. She knew he was already heavily into his workday, so decided to send him a detailed email explaining more about the puzzling happenings since she arrived in Deep Lake. She would call him later to answer his questions. At least she would try – McKenzie herself didn't know the answers to many of her own questions.

One of those questions was bothering her a lot, and it was basically why was she not missing Michael? Instead of watching for his texts, she found herself resenting them, and had been putting off calling him back.

She and Michael had had a professional and personal relationship for almost four years. They were somewhat relaxed with each other and certainly accustomed. They didn't live together but did spend most evenings together and some nights. They had the same interests and the same friends in

New York. There was something about knowing someone else's actions and responses that was familiar, if not restful. They seemed to have been drifting toward marriage but hadn't really talked about it. The word 'love' had never been exchanged, and McKenzie was puzzled about that. She didn't really know how true love felt and wondered if she ever would. Was love something that only happened to other people?

For some reason, after returning to Deep Lake, McKenzie realized that she missed being truly comfortable in her own life and in her relationships. The term "somewhat relaxed" in relation to Michael was especially troubling. He was handsome and charming, and other women shot envious glances when they went out together. At six-foot-four, with shiny black hair, dark snapping eyes, and expensive suits that fit his well-shaped manly form like a dream, he was the perfect escort and had always treated her beautifully. But. There's that word, but.

She was coming to appreciate how much she enjoyed the amazingly comfortable, steady, and reliable feelings that coursed through her when she was with her old friend Otis. Seeing the deep love between Otis and his wife troubled her in comparison to her relationship with Michael. The rapport and caring she saw in her friend's marriage was totally new to her, and she had to face the reality that these qualities were completely missing in her own relationship.

After meeting and beginning to know more about gentle and kind Ethan Thompson for the extremely short time she'd been in Deep Lake, she was beginning to wonder if her priorities were changing. Was it time to see what else might be out in the world for her? Could the terrible death of her father be the catalyst she didn't understand was waiting to pull her back to her roots?

Enough of the melancholy, McKenzie chided herself. She needed to start on the dreaded task of looking at her father's things. William should have a say about what to do with their father's clothing and personal items, also, and she must call him.

Before losing her courage, she called for William at home. Dolly answered formally and said that William was at his office, of course. McKenzie swallowed and said, "Dolly, I'm sorry that you weren't happy with our father's will. There's really nothing I can do about that, but I hope I haven't done anything to upset you. I want to do whatever I can to get our relationship on track. Frankly, I'd also like to get to know my beautiful niece. Sophie was only two when I left Deep Lake. She's already eighteen years old and I'd love to know what she's planning to do with her life."

"That's good of you to say, McKenzie. I must tell you that we were extremely disappointed about the terms of your father's will. I was shocked at the rigid stipulations he imposed on William, and I had no idea James could be so cruel."

McKenzie mentally cringed at Dolly's comment about her father but held her tongue.

Dolly continued, "We've hardly had time to think about what the repercussions will be. Sophie was planning to join Ward Transport after college, as we assumed the company would be going to William because he has worked there for a long time and certainly has a vested interest. After hearing the provisions of the will, we don't know what to think now. Sophie will be going to Carleton College in Northfield and she'll be moving into her dorm in only a few weeks."

In spite of the comment about her father being cruel, McKenzie was pleased that Dolly had thawed enough to speak to her at least, but surprised that Sophie was thinking of joining the trucking company. After minimal additional polite conversation, McKenzie suggested they meet for dinner in a few days. Dolly was happy to hear her suggestion and her manner definitely warmed. They decided to meet at the Elmo Inn in nearby Lake Elmo on Tuesday evening, and Dolly said the food was as good as it had been for many years.

"Whew," McKenzie thought after the call, "the ice is broken." At least they could meet on neutral ground and maybe begin a friendlier relationship.

She had no sooner put down the phone when William called to say he would be by later that afternoon to look at their father's personal effects. He didn't sound hopeful, but then he never did when speaking with McKenzie.

Relieved and pleased to at least hear from her brother, McKenzie realized she needed to start going through the house to see what items William might want. She started in the master bedroom and was relieved to see that her mother's things had been taken away. She had been reluctant to even enter the room earlier but found it easier somehow to know it was only men's clothes and articles she'd have to deal with. She started pulling clothes from closets and drawers and piling them all on the big bed.

Before long, Otis, in his starched uniform, arrived with lunch, and found McKenzie deep in a closet looking through a box of old photos of her family. Her face was smudged with tears and dust. Her hand was hovering over a plaster cast of that same hand in kindergarten size.

"A Deep Lake Elementary School tradition," Otis observed quietly with a small smile. "I remember the day we made our hand casts, do you?"

McKenzie sighed with mock annoyance. "Of course. Your big-toe-addition didn't add much to mine. I had to do it over."

"It sorta looked like you had a big fat sixth finger." He gazed curiously over her shoulder. "Suppose it's too much to hope that one's in there also?"

"Too much to hope," she confirmed wryly, handing him the box. "I seem to remember the one with the big toe somehow got broken – on purpose." They both laughed.

He moved to set the box on the bed. "These are special. Mary Jo has mine stored in a memory box up in the attic, and the boys' casts are hanging on our kitchen wall."

She rose to her feet with a stretch. "Let me tell ya, sometimes it's hard to match little Otis the scamp, with adult Otis the proud family man and deputy sheriff."

He flashed a broad grin. "Yeah, it's a crazy world."

McKenzie cleaned up a little while Otis headed downstairs to put their lunch together. Over lunch, she told him about dinner plans with William and Dolly and Sophia, and he nodded. "That's a good thing. Maybe you can start over on a better foundation. It looks like you'll be here a little longer, right?"

"I told my … Michael, and my office that I'd be here at least another week. I hope we can make some progress on things by then. I don't know what to think anymore. Part of me says I should sell the house and be clear of it all, but another part of me says to chuck everything in New York and come back here and settle in. It just doesn't seem reasonable, but I'm torn. I know I've only been back here for a few days and it's crazy for me to feel that way. What do you think I should do?"

"That's a dangerous question. You know what my answer would be. The longer you're here, I've been watching you become more and more like the old Kenzie I knew and loved. It's been less than a week and you're already speaking Deep Lake, whether you know it or not."

They laughed because he had heard her say "that's a whole-nother thing," when someone asked her something after the funeral the day before.

Otis continued, "I think we both know it's too early to make such a big decision. Let's start with the dilemma we have about your dad."

"Good idea. What do you think happened?"

"I wish I knew. As Ethan told you, we've looked everyplace we can imagine where those wasps could have come from when they attacked James. It was visibly obvious, and the autopsy proved he died from wasp sting and the coroner identified every sting. That's why we allowed the funeral and cremation to proceed."

"Thank you for that. So his death was natural?"

"Exactly. The problem here is that Ethan and I still have suspicions about it. We want to find out where those wasps came from. We've checked with local beekeepers to learn about wasp behavior, and they all say we should have found some sort of evidence of a nest. As you know now, we couldn't find anything in the area where he was stung except a few days later we found a very small beginning of a paper wasp nest in a nearby tree. It was way too small for the number of stings on James. One of the beekeepers said it looked like the wasps might have been 'introduced' to the area and were starting to make a new nest."

"What do you mean, 'introduced'?"

"That's the tricky part. What he meant is that someone could have brought a bunch of wasps from somewhere else, and they were starting to make a new nest in this new area."

"Oh great, so how does somebody transport a bunch of wasps?"

"Good question. I've learned it could be done by keeping the wasps cold. Not frozen, but cold – like in a refrigerator. After only a couple of hours in a refrigerator, the wasps would become docile and sluggish and you could do anything with them."

"That is scary."

"It certainly is. Because James was standing where he was when he was stung, I'm now thinking the wasps might have been somewhere in the car – like his tackle box. They could have been put in the box during the night and when James opened it that morning, they would have been warmed and awake and mad as hell."

"Oh no! Do you think that's really what happened?"

"It sounds crazy, I know, but I've been mulling it over and talking with a really knowledgeable beekeeper, and we worked out that scenario. I think it could really have happened that way."

"So now the problem is to find out who could have transported the wasps. I mean who would know enough about wasps to do such a thing? Do you have any ideas?"

"That's what I'm working on now. Your dad was a judge for a long time. There is potential for some resentful individuals in the area who might believe they were sent to prison or reprimanded by the court unfairly. Any number of them might be out now and seeking revenge, or even instructing someone on the outside to do such a thing for them while they are still incarcerated."

"What a terrible thing. I'm having trouble even thinking that someone would want to harm my dad."

"I agree, but as loved as James was around here, we have to face the fact there are some out there who may not feel that way. I believe someone did this in much the way I've worked it out. I'm keeping this quiet for now and doing as much inquiry as I can. I've been talking with the Washington County Sheriff about this, and I have his permission to pursue this as I'm able. He will provide us with the help we need as we get closer to finding who is responsible.

"You could help, too, by keeping your eyes open for anyone who strikes you as odd or maybe just insincere about your dad's death. Think you can do that?"

"Of course I can, Otis. Of course I can." McKenzie mumbled as she searched her mind for people she had seen or met in the past few days.

CHAPTER 12
CLEANING OUT

Otis and McKenzie were interrupted by the doorbell when William arrived. He and Otis shook hands and Otis left because he had to get back to work. William was not as gruff as he was before and now seemed merely sad.

"Well," he said, "it seems like every time we see each other something terrible has happened. The last time I saw you, Mom died, and everything was in a horrible mess. Now this, and it's even worse. Is it your fault?"

"Oh come on Will, be reasonable. I'm sorry you're not happy about Dad's will. You know I had nothing to do with that. We're brother and sister. Let's try to get along well enough to deal with whatever has to be done now. I miss them, too, you know, more than I can say."

"Yeah, I hear you. I just wish Dad hadn't done this stupid thing with the company. I try, I really do. I just get so caught up with other things that take time. Dolly and I talked about it and I'm going to try to spend more time at the office and get more into selling. I have to admit that Ed does a good job of running things. Because of that, I'm free to do more of what I want to do. Dolly really wants me to own and run the company. Even Sophie is talking about working there after college. She's good at numbers and it might even work for her to take over from Ed down the line."

"Will, that's more than you've said to me in twenty years. I appreciate your being open about this. Everything is so new and raw right now. Let's put it all on the shelf and deal with things as they come, okay?"

"I'm okay with that. What are you gonna do with the house – and the dog?"

"I don't know yet. That's new and raw, too, but I'm working on it. Is there anything you want of Dad's? I've pulled out all his clothes and shoes and things upstairs. I've only glanced in the garage. There must be a ton of stuff in there."

"I'm still so mad at Dad about the will, I don't want to think about it, but if you insist, I'll go look at his stuff. You didn't want anything after Mom died except for a few pieces of her jewelry, so Dolly and I gave everything to charity. Maybe that's what we should do now, too."

"You're right. What about all the fishing and hunting stuff? I expect that's in the garage."

"You can give that stuff to Ethan Thompson or Jake Connor. They were pretty close to Dad and fished together a lot. Otherwise, maybe ask Otis. He might know who to give it to. That's never been my bag – fishing and hunting. I've always been a sports guy, and I find fishing a giant bore."

McKenzie sighed and they both went upstairs to see what was there.

It didn't take long for William to pick out a set of cufflinks or two, but he wasn't interested in any of his father's clothing. It wouldn't fit him anyway as he was built differently than James had been. He wasn't interested in the pictures either, that McKenzie had pulled out of the closet. He said he and Dolly had all the pictures and junk they wanted.

They went back downstairs and William gave McKenzie the name of a charity that would pick up everything to be donated. He told her all of the furniture and any artworks in the house belonged to her now and he didn't want anything anyway. After a grunt that meant goodbye, and a glance at Goldie in the corner, he left by the kitchen door.

"Whew. That's done, thank God," McKenzie thought. She then looked at Goldie and found it strange that she had stayed quietly in the corner the whole time William was there. She never got up to greet him or nuzzle for pats or do anything friendly as McKenzie had already learned she usually did when visitors came. "Odd," she puzzled.

Greatly relieved, McKenzie pulled on one of her father's old sweaters which was hanging by the door. July day or not, she was chilled and it could be cool in the garage where she was determined to go right away to get the task over. The sweater felt good and she would go upstairs later and pull out a couple more of her dad's sweaters or jackets just to have something that belonged to him.

She took Goldie with her as she headed out to the garage. "Better to get this over with right now. There might be some boxes out there to pack up the clothes and stuff," she thought.

The original carriage house built with the house more than 150 years ago had been updated and now had double garage doors with an automatic door opener. She opened both of the big doors facing the alley with a switch inside the smaller door close to the house. Better to let in light and see what she was dealing with, she reasoned. There was one car in the garage, the newer model 4-wheel drive SUV she had noticed the other day. It was bright red, McKenzie noted with a chuckle, "Good for Dad."

There was a lawnmower, and the rest of the first floor of the building was filled with neat shelving holding boxes, planting pots, tools for various needs, fishing and hunting equipment. It was the expected detritus of living in a place for more than forty years as her parents had done. There was a second floor, which she remembered playing in when she was young, but she ignored the steep steps going up. That was a project for another day. In fact, the whole garage would have to wait until she could face it all. She found a pile of empty boxes like they were waiting for her and hauled them into the house.

She spotted her cell phone on the kitchen counter and saw a couple of texts from Michael. Tired and dirty, she decided she had enough work for the day. She took the phone out to her now-favorite spot on the yard swing while Goldie limped along, and called Michael.

"Yeah," Michael answered. "I saw your email. Are you gonna stay there now?"

"Hi to you, too, Michael. I just don't know at this point. I'm working on clearing out my father's clothes and things now, and it's a dreadful job. I miss you and I miss everything about New York, but there's something that's holding me here. I can't go into all of it now, but I'm asking you to understand. Please."

"I know this has to be hard for you, but you know real estate – it's your life. Can't you just sell the house and everything and get back here? There must be somebody you could put in charge of dealing with it all so you can come back home. I want you here."

"No, I can't. It's not that simple. I know I said I'd be another week, but it will likely be longer. There are things I can't delegate to others, and I need to be here to handle what's happening."

"I can't believe this! It's like you're throwing *us* away."

"Michael, *my father died*. I am a mess. Things here are a mess. Don't you get that? Don't you feel anything?"

"I never even met the man. Excuse me for not falling apart."

"I mean, don't you feel anything for *me*?"

"It's not like you to be clingy, complaining. Do you hear yourself, McKenzie?"

"It's not like you to be cold and demanding." Or was it? Had she learned to make allowances for his dictatorial behavior? Had she really been so foolish?

"We have an arrangement that works—or did."

Was he threatening her with a breakup now? His callous behavior was unbelievable. Suddenly, she wondered if she ever really knew the real Michael. "Look, it's best that I hang up now before I—"

"Before what?"

Before she flipped out, that's what. On that, McKenzie hit the disconnect button.

Frustrated and exhausted, she dissolved in tears. Goldie leaned against her and the two of them huddled together until darkness settled in. Finally, McKenzie went into the house and fixed Goldie's meal and a fried egg for herself.

Amid boxes and dirt, she trudged up the stairs and fell into her old bed, turning her mind off until morning.

CHAPTER 13
MEETING ISABELLA

Saturday dawned bright and filled with sunshine again. McKenzie had had a good night's sleep but awoke feeling sad and slightly forlorn after Michael's lack of support. Her mind was filled with thoughts of how to find her father's killer. Killer. What a shocking thought. She could hardly bring herself to think the word in connection with her strong and competent father. Funny thing about fathers. They just seem to be there, without fanfare, without pomp and circumstance. They're just there in the background until you need them, and then suddenly they're not.

After a good run and Goldie chores, she showered and felt like a new woman. She brought up the empty boxes and started filling them with stuff for charity. Pulling out an old jacket and a couple more sweaters of her dad's to keep, she packed up everything, including some fine-looking suits. With many trips up and down, she hauled it all out to the garage, where the charity van could pick up what would be given away. The boxes of pictures were set aside and would go in the attic when she could bring herself to go up there. That was a project needing more time, she realized.

The master bedroom closet and dresser drawers were empty and the whole room looked lonely. "Hmmm," she thought, "maybe I should move in here – my old room is much smaller. I guess I might as well be comfortable for as long as

I'm here." There were several other rooms along the second-floor hall, but none of them appealed to her. It might just work to move into her parents' old room, and the more she thought about it, the better the idea sounded. I'll move later, she decided when she stole a glance at her watch and remembered Ethan and his daughter were coming over in just a few hours. That gave her time to make a run to the grocery store for some staples.

*****

Back from the store, she parked the rental car behind the garage and off the alley. She'd been leaving it in front of the house on the street and that seemed silly now. In fact, now that she was the owner of a nice new SUV, why not return the rental car? She'd think more about that later and headed upstairs to clean up for the special visit.

Ready early, she guiltily did a little work on the computer with her New York office and before long, the front doorbell rang.

"Hello, McKenzie." Ethan was as friendly as before, and she now realized why the gals at the beauty shop were so impressed with him. He really was good looking, and he didn't seem to know it. He was wearing old jeans and a comfortable shirt that hadn't seen an iron ever. His brown hair was well-cut and those warm brown eyes looked like they could melt steel. He was about six feet tall and muscular, but not overly so. His smile was genuine, and he had a couple of crooked bottom teeth that just added charm.

The young girl at his side looked up and said, "Hi, I'm Isabella. I'm five, and I'm tall." She was dressed in jeans and a tee-shirt, with some sparkly sandals that seemed a little out of character.

McKenzie leaned in closer to the child's level with bright eyes. "Yes, I see that you're tall for being five. I'm McKenzie, and I'm older than five, but I'm sort of tall, too. I see you've got blond hair, and I do, too. Do you like dogs?"

"Oh, yes, I like most dogs, but I love Goldie," Isabella cried as she ran into the kitchen and wrapped her arms around Goldie's neck. Goldie was wagging her body and making whimpers of happiness as the little girl hugged and petted her.

Ethan was grinning and the love for his daughter shone all over his face. "It looks like Goldie is feeling much better today. Thank you, Isabella, for being gentle with her. You're taking good care of her, McKenzie," he said.

"I think we're taking care of each other, to be honest," she replied. "Being responsible for Goldie is helping me to deal with everything that has happened. We're best friends by now."

"I was hoping that would happen, and it's not a surprise. We didn't know if you had a checkers game, so we brought one along. Do you play checkers?"

"I certainly do. It's one of my favorites but I haven't played in a long time. I hope you'll be patient with me."

Isabella answered charmingly, "I'll try to be patient. That's something my daddy is teaching me. He said that when God was handing out patience, I was behind the door and didn't get my share. But we're working on it."

They all laughed and McKenzie and Isabella headed for the dining room table for playing checkers. The two of them played the first couple of games while Ethan checked out Goldie's foot.

Ethan was pleased with how well the foot was healing. He was still puzzled that they couldn't find out how the foot got cut, but Goldie seemed to be doing better than he expected.

Isabella beat McKenzie soundly in the first game and cheered loudly as she captured her last king. The second game was quieter as McKenzie remembered a little more about playing. Isabella still beat her and actually told her that she played better that time. McKenzie won the third game and Isabella said, "Now you're getting it!"

"What a precocious child, and she's very mature for her age," McKenzie thought. "She doesn't sulk if she doesn't win, and I can see Ethan's kindness in her." It was altogether a fun afternoon.

"We were thinking of going for a ride, Kenzie," Ethan said with a glance at his watch and slipped into the easier nickname that Otis used. "Care to join us?"

"Actually, you could help me out. With Dad's perfectly good SUV in the garage, it seems silly to keep my rental car. Would you mind following me to the airport and giving me a lift back?"

"And see airplanes take off?" Isabella asked with a bright look.

Ethan nodded. "We're sure to see a few."

On the way back from the airport, where Ethan patiently parked for almost an hour so Isabella could watch several of the big planes take off, he asked, "We're thinking of going out for some pizza, and we'd love to have you join us. Is that okay with you, Kenzie?"

"I'd love it. Where to?"

"We've got a favorite place in Stillwater. It's not far and their pizza is great. What do you like on your pizza?"

"Well, pretty much everything except anchovies. How about you?"

Isabella squealed, "That's just what we like, too! Anchovies are yukky!" The girls did a high-five over the seat-back, where Isabella still sat in the back of the car in her booster seat.

Over pizza, McKenzie learned that Ethan had lived in Milwaukee, Wisconsin, but his grandma lived in Deep Lake and had needed help in her later years. Ethan and his wife Elizabeth moved to Minnesota and he started his veterinary practice. His grandmother passed away while they lived in Deep Lake. The small family stayed in Ethan's grandmother's house which he had inherited. Shortly after Isabella was born, Elizabeth developed an extremely fast-growing cancer and she died when Isabella was very young, which was devastating for all of them. Elizabeth's mother had also moved to Minnesota while her daughter was ill and now lived in Edina, a stylish Minneapolis suburb.

McKenzie watched Isabella carefully to see how she was doing with the conversation about her mother. She was sad and somewhat downcast through the telling, but McKenzie admired the compassionate way Ethan told the story. She could see Isabella had no memory of her mother. She was just too young when she died, but she seemed to pretend for her dad's sake, and that wasn't all bad.

To pick up the mood a little, McKenzie asked Isabella, "I understand you just finished kindergarten. Would you like to tell me about how it was? It's been such a long time that I was in kindergarten, I'm sure it has changed a lot since then."

It was the perfect way to move the conversation along, and all three of them chatted and laughed through the pizza.

Ethan walked McKenzie to her door when they got to her house, and Isabella waited in the car after a sweet hug. Again, he took her hands and looked into her eyes, saying, "Thank you for a beautiful and uncomplicated day, Kenzie. I hope you don't mind if I call you by the nickname Otis uses. You are truly special, and I don't think you even know how special."

Later, in bed, McKenzie relived the day in her memory. Ethan was definitely growing on her. This had been their first real date – or sort of anyway, and she realized she liked him more each time she saw him. She fell asleep smiling, something she hadn't done for a very long time, and she didn't even know it.

CHAPTER 14

SETTLING IN

Sunday dawned a little overcast, but they needed rain, McKenzie thought. "Here I go again, I'm not just speaking Deep Lake, but thinking it, too." She hadn't thought about needing rain for half her lifetime, but now she was thinking about the flowers lining the walk and they were looking thirsty yesterday.

She decided to go to church that morning. She enjoyed Pastor Osterholt at the funeral and was curious about how good a sermon he could preach. The thought surprised her because McKenzie hadn't gone to church since she left Deep Lake. Somehow it felt right to go now, and she rushed through the morning chores to get there at nine as they had only one service through the summer.

She found the keys to the SUV and raised the garage door. Driving her dad's car for the first time was a challenge. She didn't think about it being where her father had died, or that it was his car at all; she jumped right in and after getting familiar with the gadgets and features, she drove it like a pro getting to church right on time. She hadn't driven much during the past sixteen years and found now that she enjoyed it. Her dad had good taste in cars and this one was fine for her.

McKenzie was greeted by many people at church, some of whom she had seen at the funeral. She didn't know if William and Dolly were churchgoers or not, and that was their choice.

It felt good to her to be there and the sermon was pretty good as well. She stayed for coffee after the church service and visited more with others, including Otis and his family. Even Janice and Vicky were there, and they mingled with others as though they were regulars. McKenzie wondered briefly if the church people knew that Vicky was once a boy. "Doesn't matter," she contemplated to herself, "but all the better if they know and it doesn't change how they accept Vicky."

Janice and Vicky found out that McKenzie wasn't leaving that day as she had planned previously, and they were happy with the news. They made a date for the following evening to have crazy cocktails at the new place in town. McKenzie was thrilled and eager to be with her old friends and was looking forward to the time out.

Later in the afternoon, Pastor Osterholt came over as he had said he would. McKenzie was glad to see him and hoped she could learn a little more about how the town had changed while she had been away. She asked about William and Dolly, and he told her frankly they were good givers but very seldom showed up for services.

The two of them had an open conversation about the difficulties in dealing with her father's death. She opened up and talked about her dilemma of possibly moving back to Deep Lake and living in her parents' house, which was now hers, of course. He gave her a good piece of advice, which was to make a list of pros and cons for staying in Deep Lake or going back to New York. He told her to put everything on the list, including likes and dislikes, job issues, gut feelings, and possibilities, and to study the list carefully before making such a big decision.

After a brief and thoughtful prayer, the pastor was leaving, and McKenzie said, "Thank you so much for coming, Pastor. I had no idea I would appreciate your visit so much. Young as you are, you are a wise man, and I'm glad you're at Hope Lutheran. You gave me good advice and I will think hard on it."

Pastor Osterholt answered, "I love this little town, and thank you so much for your kind words. It's not perfect, but no place is. The people here need me, and I believe I'm where I'm supposed to be right now. God bless you in your tough decision-making," he said as he headed out the door.

*****

McKenzie spent the afternoon moving into her new house's master bedroom. It had a nice view of the lawn and street in front of the house, an attached bathroom, and it felt right. Thanks to Otis's dad, Al, the walls were nicely painted and even when she moved the furniture a little, there were no shadows or spots on the walls and the neutral color was fine with her. Even the neutral colored carpet was fairly new and didn't need to be changed. Her dad had done a good job of keeping things up in the house, she mused.

There wasn't much to move, so with a little time on her hands, she dug through the boxes of pictures she had moved to the attic stairway and reminisced about growing up here. The box contained pictures of all her family at various stages of their lives, including school photos for every year for both William and McKenzie. William was good-looking from childhood on, and he mugged his school pictures. Her pictures were just plain messy looking. Braces helped her crooked teeth in junior high, but it took a long time for her hair to look decent. It was unruly and never seemed to hang right. In later high school she learned that cutting her hair short was the best look for her and she had kept it that way ever since.

She uncovered a picture of the seventh-grade football team. In those days her hair was blond and fine and feathery and stuck out in every direction, so she wore baseball caps most of the time. She also wore jeans and baggy shirts, and pretty much looked like a boy. After all, her best friend was a boy, and she did what Otis did. Many of the kids called her "Ken" in those days, and the seventh-grade football coach thought she was a boy when she went out for the team. She didn't correct him and played almost the whole season on the boy's football team. Her mother went to a game one day and happened to ask the coach if he knew she was a girl. That was the end of her football career. She joined the tennis team instead and did okay with that. She and Otis became quite competitive in tennis, eventually. She wondered if he still played.

Memories washed over her in waves while she looked through the box of old photos. Someone took a snap of her and Otis ice fishing. Bundled from top to bottom with only their smiles showing, they proudly held up their catch. McKenzie remembered the incident of finding the body under the ice. They were about ten then, and she wondered whatever happened afterward. They heard the man's name – Antonini something, she thought, and he was some sort of bad guy, but it was all a blur now. Her dad kept the details away from her so she would not be upset, as he put it. She was curious, but let it go for her dad's sake, and then eventually forgot about the whole incident. She and Otis participated in the ice fishing contests for several years after that happened. They may have thought about it now and then, but other years and other catches won their memories.

Pictures of her mom and dad brought tears, and McKenzie decided it was time to put the boxes away. Today might be a good time to do a little shopping. She needed some casual clothes, and Maplewood Shopping Center was not far away.

Goldie's foot was much better now, and Ethan had taken the bandages off Saturday. She still limped a little, but it healed more every day. Her daily routine was getting more and more established and comfortable for both of them. When she'd be gone a short time, McKenzie left Goldie in the fenced-in backyard with plenty of water and a cool spot to rest. McKenzie got ready for her small shopping spree, patted Goldie goodbye, and took off for the mall with plans to work on her "pro and con" list when she returned.

*****

Unknown to McKenzie as she pulled out of the alley outside her garage on her way to Maplewood Mall, a dirty gray pickup pulled out of a side street and followed her. A lone man was in the pickup. He followed her to the mall, waited for her to do her shopping, and followed her back to the house, parking a couple of blocks away. Oblivious to what just happened, McKenzie parked the car back in the garage and went in the kitchen door with her purchases and the dog.

*****

Some new jeans and shorts, a trio of relaxed pullovers, and a pair of attractive but comfortable sandals made up the bulk of her shopping, but a Liz Claiborne outfit of capris and a matching top in shades of blue had caught her eye, also. It might be good for the night on the town with Janice and Vicky.

Pleased with her purchases, she stowed them away and sat in the kitchen with a pad and pencil. "Odd," she thought, "I didn't even think of using the computer for my pro and con lists. Somehow paper and pencil works best for this."

She started with the pros and mulled over the reasons for her to choose to stay in Deep Lake or go back to New York. She decided that deep thinking would only muddy the waters, and quick, off-the-cuff, ideas might work better. She wrote:

Pros:

- Can help with finding out if somebody killed my dad.
- Like the house.
- Can keep Goldie.
- I'm making friends here (Mary Jo and more).
- Feel comfortable being back home (wow, "home" is how I'm thinking about it).
- Could sell my business to Desiree.
- Could sell real estate in the eastern suburbs of the Twin Cities to make some income.
- Don't really need much income with my investments and savings.

Cons:

- Michael won't like it.
- It's a big change.

- I would be leaving a business that makes a lot of money.
- Leaving friends … (what friends? They're all basically business acquaintances.)
- Have to sell my apartment.
- Michael won't like it.

Michael. With a big sigh, she went back to the "pro" list and added, "I'd like to know Ethan better."

McKenzie looked over her lists and sighed again. The result was clearer than she expected. A final decision was going to take more than lists.

Tired and confused, she called it a night and crawled into the big bed in her new room. Comforted by the thought that her parents slept here together, she fell asleep instantly.

Some time later, McKenzie was wakened by a ringing phone. She sleepily looked around for her cell, which she had again left downstairs in the kitchen. An extension of the house phone was sitting on the bedside table and ringing impatiently. She grabbed it and offered a tentative, "H-hello?"

"Get outta our town. We don't want you here!" said a raspy voice, and immediately hung up.

Wide awake and sputtering, McKenzie sat up and stared at the phone. "Who was that?" she cried and instinctively clutched the blanket to her chest. Thinking more rationally, she ran downstairs in the pajamas she had worn as a teenager, to make sure the doors were locked. They were, and everything looked quiet as she peeked out the windows. Goldie sat up in surprise as McKenzie sharply pulled the shades down in the kitchen. Still frantic, but beginning to calm down, she realized it was two in the morning. Everything seemed as usual outside. Goldie didn't seem alarmed, so she decided to wait until morning to call Otis.

McKenzie had noticed that Goldie never left the kitchen. Apparently, her dad had trained her to not go into the rest of the house and she didn't ever cross the doorway into the dining or living rooms. When Ethan and Isabella had been there, and they played games in the dining room, Goldie laid in the kitchen doorway with her chin on the carpet beyond, but she didn't venture out of the room. Now, McKenzie grabbed Goldie's collar and almost dragged her with her up the stairs to her room. Reluctantly, Goldie followed and once there, laid down carefully beside the bed.

McKenzie had also snatched her cell phone and took it with her upstairs. Looking under the bed, she saw a ball bat which might have served as "protection" for her parents in case of an intruder. She pulled it out and climbed back into bed armed with the bat and her cell phone. She looked down at a slightly nervous Goldie and thought about the call, which was by this time almost becoming a bad dream. She knew she should call Otis about it, but everything was quiet now and it was late, so she decided to wait until morning. Goldie settled down and went to sleep. While wondering who it could have been and thinking of possibilities, McKenzie eventually fell back to sleep, too.

CHAPTER 15
MONDAY

McKenzie called Otis on Monday morning while he was on his first cup of coffee at his office. "I think we need to talk more about what's going on. Can you come over?"

"Whoa, what's up so early?" he sputtered.

"I had a phone call in the middle of the night that wasn't friendly."

"I'll be right there."

True to his word, fifteen minutes later Otis was sitting in McKenzie's kitchen with a fresh cup of better coffee. She had already filled him in on what happened during the night and they were in deep discussion. The house phone's digital readout showed only that a call came from "St. Paul," most likely from a prepaid cell phone which would not be traceable.

"Your dad was a judge for many years. There are bound to be people out there who feel they were given a bad rap for whatever reason. I've been looking at this since James's death, and have already identified a few to look at more closely. Some people have a warped sense of what's right. I've been a law officer for fifteen years now, and I'm continually surprised by the crazy things people do because they think they've been wronged, whether it's true or not."

"I guess you're right about that. It just doesn't make sense to me. Why can't people just live and let live, as the saying goes?" a frustrated and weary McKenzie replied.

"Please don't let this scare you away, Kenzie. It is a serious thing, yes, but we'll get to the bottom of it, I promise you."

"No way will it scare me away. If anything, it makes me more determined to stay and see this thing through. I want to find out what happened to my dad. The majority of people here respected and loved him. I know this from the way they've spoken to me since I've been here. I have to tell you, Otis, that I'm thinking seriously of staying in Deep Lake."

"No kidding? That's great!"

"I've been in New York a long time. To be honest, it feels like I've done what I can there in business. It was good, don't get me wrong, and I'm pretty much at the top of my game there as far as competition and reputation go. But. There's that word again. But. I've discovered something back here in Deep Lake I didn't know I was missing. There's a closeness and a sense of well-being here that I didn't appreciate when I was young. I like it now, and the longer I'm here, the less I want to give it up."

"That's awesome! What happened to change your mind?"

"I had a good conversation with Erik Osterholt about some pros and cons about the whole thing, and once I sat down and started looking at them, it became clear this is where I really want to be. I can't deny it."

"What about your fiancé back in New York, and your business?"

"I need to work all of that out, of course, and it won't be easy. As far as Michael goes, I see now our relationship has been based more on business than on love. I'm seeing more clearly what real love actually looks like, and, to be blunt, ours doesn't measure up. I hope I can make him understand that, too."

"Wow. Sounds like you've got your work cut out for you. Can I tell Mary Jo? She'll be thrilled, as I am, for sure."

"Yes, of course, you can tell Mary Jo. She's a big part of my decision if you want to know, and you are, too. But please don't tell anyone else yet. I want to take this slowly and get some answers to what happened to Dad, first of all."

"You got it. I'm going back to the office to check out this caller, but I doubt if I'll get anywhere on it for now. Meanwhile, I'll keep working on those leads of guys who might feel unjustly imprisoned or misjudged. If anything else happens like last night, call me right away. That's my job, you know."

"I will. I've got Goldie sleeping upstairs with me now and that feels good, even if she'd probably lick an intruder to death if anything."

"There's more. I'm sorry that I forgot to mention it, but James had a permit for a small gun. I think he kept the gun in the back of the drawer next to his bed. Check it out and I'll get you an application form for Minnesota. It takes about a week for them to check you out, and then you can do the required training and practice shots in as little as a day at the main Washington County sheriff's department in Stillwater. I'd feel better if you had control of something to protect you, the way things are going."

"Good advice. I have a small gun in my apartment in New York. You can't be too careful in New York, so I've had one for years. I'll check out Dad's gun and see which one I like better, in case I want to bring mine back."

Getting ready to leave, Otis put his hands on her shoulders. "I'm so glad you'll be staying here, Kenzie. I believe it's the right thing for you now, and it would sure make us happy. Who knows, you might find the right someone to settle down with and have a whole herd of kids to make life more interesting."

"Yeah, sure, anything to increase the population of Deep Lake." McKenzie remarked.

"We're on this whole mystery, Kenzie. I mean it. Call me right away if anything else out of the ordinary happens."

"You bet I will. Thanks for all you're doing and thanks for just being you."

Later, McKenzie found the small handgun in the side table drawer where Otis thought it might be. She forgot to look in the drawer while moving in the room, and there it was, plain as day. It was a Ruger LCRx .38 Special and looked fairly new. She did a little research online and discovered that LCR stands for "Lightweight Carry Revolver," and it had a reduced friction trigger system. She would text Otis to see if he thought this might work for her. It certainly looked more appropriate than the Beretta she left back in New York. A boyfriend prior to Michael chose it and it was heavier and clumsier to hold. Hoping she would never have to hold this one after the firing range test, she put it back in the drawer. "What a scary world we've created," she thought, "that I even have to consider having such a thing in my house."

*****

Deciding to hold off talking with Michael, or Denise at her New York office, she spent the day combing around the house for more things to put in the garage for charity pickup. The basement was another treasure trove of memories as well as useful items for someone else. She found no fewer than three food processors, something her dad must not have liked, plus two old vacuum cleaners that appeared to work. There were a couple of coffee makers, several unused tables and many knick-knacks. There were boxes of travel maps that her dad had been storing for years. In fact, they were all from before her mother died, which made them even sadder. Her dad didn't travel much at all that she knew of in the years since her mother's death. It looked like he lost interest without his beloved Rose to travel with him.

She heard the upstairs house phone ring and rushed to get it. It was Janice, confirming their date that night at the sports bar. She pushed her dusty hand through her hair and agreed to meet at six and tore off for the shower. She also thought she needed a couple more sets of hands-free phones with her house-phone number. Might as well keep the number her family had used since she was tiny. Cell phones were good and convenient, but she didn't like carrying one around in the house. She was already in the habit of leaving it plugged in in the kitchen when she was puttering around in the house. Another pro for staying in Deep Lake? She had found she liked puttering around and realized all she did in her New York apartment was sleep. Hmmmm.

*****

The evening at the sports bar was fun and filled with laughter, just what McKenzie needed after the past week of stress. She wore her new Liz Claiborne outfit and it fit in with what others were wearing. Her new sandals were comfortable and looked good, too. Janice and Vicky were filling her in on years of innocent gossip and stories. McKenzie had missed this about a small town. The gossip wasn't malicious – it was just informative and matter of fact. What a change from New York. McKenzie couldn't help but compare the stories shared over cocktails in Manhattan that bordered on being catty to just plain mean. The stories in Deep Lake had an undercurrent of kindness and concern for someone experiencing difficulties or troubles.

After a couple of hours – and a couple of cocktails apiece, they had gone through the list of most of their classmates – what they were doing and where they were at this point in their lives. Who married whom, and who had divorced whom, and who was the most successful, and so on. McKenzie hadn't attended any class reunions over the years, and speculation about her success had long been wildly exaggerated. Many knew that she attended Cornell University in upper New York State, and continued there to earn dual Master of Business Administration/ Master of Professional Studies degrees. Not as many knew she had then gone into commercial real estate in New York City. For those who did, the stories went from her being currently penniless and managing a fleabag hotel, to being one of the richest women in New York. This was cause for much additional laughter, and she assured her friends that she had done well in her field but was far from either end of the imagined spectrum.

Well into the evening, McKenzie decided to test the waters about her dilemma of moving back to Deep Lake. She said, "Okay gals, I'm gonna drop a bomb here. What would you say if I told you I'm thinking seriously about staying in Deep Lake?"

With wide eyes and a deep gasp, Janice shouted, "No shit!?"

"Hold it down girl, I'm not completely sure yet, but I'm thinking about it."

"Well, think no longer, woman, Deep Lake needs you," Janice growled in her sensual low-toned voice.

Vicky added wistfully, "Oh just think of all the gorgeous guys who will be sniffing around you. Can I have your leftovers? I can hardly wait!"

After snickers all around, Janice said, "Speaking of guys – any progress with our mouth-watering vet, Ethan Thompson?"

"Oh, Janice. He's a really nice man and I must confess I enjoyed having pizza with him and his daughter."

"Pizza, huh, so things are moving along there?"

"I may see him again, you never know. I've got more on my plate now and I need to make some big decisions. One thing I need to think about is making a little money here. I'm tired of the commercial thing and am thinking about selling houses. What do you think about that?"

Janice replied, "There are several big real estate companies in the area and I would expect that any of them would be thrilled to have you. I have some customers who sell and I could do some discreet asking around if you want me to. Otherwise, just Google the area and call some of the bigger outfits. See what they have to say."

"Good idea. I'll check into it soon. I need to make some final decisions and have some tough conversations before I do anything more. This isn't easy."

They decided to call it a night and got ready to leave. McKenzie had determined that Vicky was much better as a woman than a man, and liked her even better than she did back in high school when Vicky was Vidal. She was more frank and straightforward and open, and that was so refreshing. Janice was smart and also wise, and McKenzie was so glad to connect again with her. Janice had never married either but said she was still looking. Her shop was successful, and she was taking care of her aging widowed mother. The two of them lived comfortably together in her childhood home.

CHAPTER 16
ENDINGS AND BEGINNINGS

Early the next morning, McKenzie went out for her usual run. Goldie wasn't yet up to tagging along, so she left her dozing in the kitchen. Jogging easily along the neighborhood sidewalks, she inhaled the invigorating air and scanned the brilliant blue sky. Everything was so crisp and clean in Deep Lake. In the city, people seldom bothered to make eye contact on the street. Within a matter of minutes she'd waved to a mailman, a fellow jogger, and a boy delivering newspapers. It felt so good to return a friendly greeting and a sincere smile. It wasn't as refreshing as a cup of morning coffee, but close to it.

Pausing at a moderately busy four-way-stop, she jogged in place as a few cars passed through. The last, a red Corolla, was proceeding slower than necessary, she noted. But there proved to be a reason, as the driver was soon hailing her with a toot of her horn. McKenzie laughed and waved back. The driver's blond hair was lighter and styled shorter than she remembered, but there was no mistaking Mrs. Wilson, the elementary school librarian. Mrs. Wilson had always liked her because McKenzie was such a diligent reader and library volunteer. Otis hadn't fared so well with the woman, once putting a tadpole in her desk drawer. His punishment had been a three-page writing assignment on tadpoles. It would be fun if Mary Jo had that research paper in Otis's memory box.

"Still at the school?" McKenzie hollered in the direction of the Corolla's open passenger window.

"You betcha!" With another toot of her horn, Mrs. Wilson was off down the street.

McKenzie was momentarily distracted by the librarian's license plate, BOOK-EM, when she stepped off the curb into the crosswalk. Suddenly, the rev of a powerful engine hammered her ears. She snapped her head around to spot a dirty gray pickup bearing down hard from the opposite direction—aiming straight at her!

Navigating the unpredictable crush of city drivers for such a long time had made her a savvy pedestrian, heightening senses and steeling her nerves. With a rush of adrenalin, she reacted swiftly to the large careening vehicle, running full force back over the curb and then the wide grassy boulevard. She tumbled behind a sturdy oak tree just in time to avoid being hit.

By the time she righted herself for a look, the truck was on its way in the direction Mrs. Wilson had taken.

Leaning against the tree trunk, McKenzie dug out her phone to call Otis. A nasty late-night call was bad enough. But this was a matter of life and death.

Otis was by her side in minutes as he was on his way to work. "Tell me what happened. Are you okay?" he asked anxiously.

"I'm okay. I was able to speed up enough to get out of the way, but it was close. Otis, who is doing this?" she cried.

They sat together on the ground and he urged her to have a drink of water from the bottle velcroed to her side. "Let's talk it out now, while it's fresh in your mind. Tell me exactly what you remember."

McKenzie related the incident about being distracted by Mrs. Wilson.

"Did you get any of the license plate?"

"Nope. It all happened way too fast. And the truck was dirty top to bottom."

"Probably intentionally dirty. Could you see anyone in the cab?"

"No, I couldn't tell anything about the driver and I don't know if there was one person or six people in it from what I could see." Her heart and breathing were calming, but her mind was full of questions. "Could it have been the person who called me in the middle of the night?"

"I don't know, Kenzie, but I'll do what I can to find out. I'm going to check with your neighbors first, to see if they've seen anything odd in the neighborhood. Meanwhile, get in my car and rest for a few minutes while I ask these folks standing around if they saw anything. Then, I'll take you home; it's not far but you're in no shape to run anymore today. I'm so thankful you got out of the way. We have to get this nightmare figured out. This can't go on."

*****

After a good cool-down stretch and a shower, McKenzie completed the form Otis gave her for registering her dad's handgun in her name. She would take it into Stillwater to the Washington County Court House later, but she needed to make some important phone contacts. This aborted attempt on her life, as she and Otis viewed the incident with the pickup, was the last straw. There was no way anyone or anything was going to make her leave Deep Lake any time soon.

She texted Desiree at her office and asked her to call back immediately. She then started putting some numbers together and prepared for making Desiree Canard one very happy woman, she expected.

Her second text was to Michael. She was blunt and to the point, as he had been in all of his texts to her in the past week. "Am staying in Deep Lake. More later." Within ten minutes, he called.

"What the hell is going on out there?" he shouted. "What do you mean, 'staying in Deep Lake?' Have you lost your mind?"

"No Michael, I think I just found it. Things have been happening fast and furious here, and I've discovered I need to make some changes in my life."

"What sort of changes?"

"There's a mystery around my dad's death, and I can't leave in the middle of trying to solve it. And it's not just that. I've come to understand there's more to life than making money, and I want to see what's out in the world for me. I've got a beautiful old house now, and a dog who needs me, and a town I want to know more about. I'm staying, Michael."

"What about our life together? I thought we had a good thing going. We've been together almost four years now. Are you just going to throw that away?"

"We're not really together, Michael. You have your place and I have mine. We come together for business and sex, and I'm realizing that's not enough for me. I want more out of life and I'm learning that New York isn't where I'm going to find it."

"So you're telling me we're finished? Just like that?" he said, sounding a little hurt.

"Yes, we're finished. Just like that. I'm sorry to be so brusque, but it doesn't make sense to draw it out. I'm finding that honesty is the only way to go here, and I can't continue living in a way that I no longer believe in. I've changed, Michael, and it's for the good."

"You sure have changed. I don't know what's going on out there in the sticks but you don't even sound like the McKenzie I know."

"I can't even go back now to close out my apartment and the business, but I'll do that down the line sometime. Maybe I'll call you when I'm there."

"Yeah, maybe. I don't think so from the sound of things. Don't expect me to be waiting. I need somebody who's here for me, just like I thought you were. I guess this is goodbye, McKenzie."

Thinking this was not as hard as she expected it to be, she said, "Yes, it is. Goodbye Michael. I wish you well with your clients. And by the way, you might tell Mavis that she left her red bra under your bed. I found it before the cleaning lady came the last time I was there. In case she's still looking for it, I threw it away." She pushed 'end call' and took a deep breath. She didn't expect to feel like a huge weight fell off her shoulders, but that's what happened.

Unconsciously smiling, her third text was to her secretary, Gayle. "Watch for email. Need help in closing up my apartment. Putting it all in storage. Am staying here. Thx."

She pounded out instructions to Gayle and Desiree in separate lengthy emails while cooling down from the conversation with Michael. There was no other way to describe it – she felt relief, loud and clear. The tough decisions had been made and there was no going back now. Gayle would take care of the apartment and send her clothes. There was very little McKenzie really cared about in the apartment, and she would deal with everything in storage when time allowed. Desiree could handle the rents from the apartment buildings McKenzie owned and the rest of the business as well for the foreseeable future. As far as her clients were concerned, Desiree could have them, and McKenzie expected she would be very happy for the privilege.

It wasn't as hard as she believed, to shut down a life. The more she thought about it, the giddier she became as she remembered it wasn't even lunchtime yet. What a morning!

Reaching down to give Goldie a pat, her house phone rang. It was Ethan.

"Are the hotdishes all gone?"

"Yup. What did you have in mind," she said with a grin.

"I'm just leaving for lunch and thought I'd pick up something for us to eat and check on Goldie once more. Okay with you?"

"It's more than okay. I'm hungry for one of Joe's hamburgers. How about picking up a take-out order and we can eat in my yard swing. I've got news for you," she answered with a wider grin.

CHAPTER 17
QUESTIONS

O tis did a quick inquiry of the few bystanders who accumulated where McKenzie had been so nearly run down, but none of them had seen anything of consequence. A couple of people saw the dirty gray truck but had no further details about it. The people were alerted only when they saw McKenzie on the ground. No one he talked with had seen what caused her to get there. When Otis went back after taking McKenzie home, he found a faint rubber mark on the street where the pickup had swerved, but it wasn't identifiable.

He then questioned neighbors in the area where McKenzie lived to see if anyone knew anything about a gray pickup. Mrs. Hoffmann, a widow who lived across the street, had seen the gray pickup parked along the street for the past couple of days. She had bad arthritis and spent a lot of time in her recliner looking out the window. She told Otis she put food for the squirrels outside on the air conditioner. While they sat there eating the food, they chattered at her like saying thank you. The squirrels entertained her for hours. She had noticed the dirty truck because it would park down the block and after a couple of hours drive away and nobody ever got in or out of it. The license plate was covered with mud or dirt as she tried once to read it but couldn't, so she just forgot about the incident until Otis came around asking.

Don Werner, who lived across the alley from McKenzie, and was a manager at the pickle factory on the edge of town, noticed McKenzie hauling stuff to the garage one day and was going to offer to help her, but before he got around to it, she drove off in her dad's SUV. Don did say he saw a dirty gray pickup drive through the alley the day before as he was taking the garbage out. He thought it was a local farmer delivering something to somebody and didn't think more about it.

Others in the area, Werner's wife, the Schmitts, Millers, and Iversons and some others, weren't much help as most of them were away working during the day or too busy to see anything odd going on. They all, however, had noticed that the judge's house looked lived in now his daughter was back, and they had seen her go running in the early mornings. In fact, several of them had taken food over to the house before the funeral and used the key above the door to put it in the kitchen. All of the neighbors had gone to James's funeral and were curious to know if McKenzie was staying in Deep Lake.

Back at his office, with a frustrated sigh at the limited information he had gathered, Otis wrote it all up. He then concentrated on looking at some of the people Judge Ward had sentenced in recent years. Otis had acquired mountains of court documents to go through, and the work was tedious. The old adage, 'needle in a haystack' came to mind as he sorted and read through volumes of information. Bleary-eyed and even more stymied at the impossibilities in the 'haystack' front of him, he had a better thought.

The next morning, Otis approached the three old men sitting outside the barbershop. He brought each of them a cup of fresh coffee along with a bag of donuts from the bakery to pass around. He pulled up a battered old folding chair that seemed to be left leaning against the side of the building for just that purpose and started talking.

"Hey guys, how you doing?" Otis started.

He was met with mumbles from chocolate-filled mouths, and one old guy with powdered sugar dusting his mustache, said, "Not bad, Otis. How's things with you?"

"Okay, Howard. I'm just looking for a little information and thought maybe you guys could help."

"Oh yeah, how could we help with anything? We don't know nothin'."

"You might know more than you think. You know that Judge Ward has died of course, and his daughter is back here for a while and living in the Judge's house."

"Oh yeah, that was too bad about the Judge. Bees, eh? What a shitty way to die."

"Yes, it sure was. He was careful about his allergy all his life but there's something odd about the whole business and some weird things have been happening since his daughter came back. I'm just poking around a little to see if anybody knows anything. I think you guys see pretty much everything that goes on in Deep Lake, right?"

The three of them looked at each other and shrugged.

"Anything goin' on that you don't feel is right these days?"

One of the guys said, "You mean that Joe's raised his price on coffee by a nickel?" They all chuckled over this.

"Well, some things we can't do anything about, Fred. I'm talking about people or vehicles that you haven't seen before or might look out of place for some reason. For example, I'm looking for an older gray pickup that's pretty dirty. You seen that around?"

"Hmm, that pretty much describes a third of the vehicles in town – farmers coming in to get supplies and all, and we've had a lotta rain this summer. Makes for a lotta mud."

"I was afraid of that," Otis said dejectedly.

The other man, old George who used to work at the lumberyard east of town, said, "There was a gray pickup the other day that I didn't recognize, now I think about it. The driver didn't wave or look at us like everybody else does, and that made me curious. He turned his head away when he went by, in fact, and I didn't get a good look at him. Downright unfriendly, he was, and that's unusual right there."

"For sure," the others agreed.

Fred added, "Did you know that Bob Winehauser's son came back from the slammer a month or so ago? I think Judge Ward put him away a few years back over some ruckus. Don't know what for sure, but I remember Bob was pretty pissed about Bobbie having to go to prison."

Otis was surprised. "No, I didn't know Bobbie was back. I usually know when people get out, but maybe my paperwork was slow and hasn't caught up with me yet. His parole officer will be someone in Stillwater, so I'll check that out. Have you guys seen Bobbie around?"

"Nah, he lives way out 'a town," Fred offered. "I ain't seen him around at all. You guys?" The others shook their heads and it appeared nobody had seen Bobbie since he got out.

Otis finished up. "Well I'll check Bobbie out just in case. Keep your eyes peeled, guys. We need to keep our town clean. See ya around."

They all nodded and Otis headed back to the office to check out Bobbie Winehauser.

*****

An hour later, Otis was surprised to get a call from Ed Johnson, manager of Ward Transport.

"I've been debating whether or not to call you, Otis. I don't know that anything can or should be done here, but I wanted to let you know about something strange that happened yesterday."

"Sure, Ed. What happened?" Under his breath, he said, "We seem to be having a run on strange things happening around here."

"Yesterday, I was on my way to work in the morning – you know I live on one of those big hills in Stillwater, on a street that goes straight up or down, depending on which way you're looking at it. Anyway, just as I was headed down the hill, my brakes failed. It was scary as hell, I have to tell you – I stomped on those brakes and there was nothing there – the car didn't even slow down. By sheer luck, I was able to steer the car into the block wall that borders on the old courthouse before I got going too fast. You know where I mean?"

"Of course I do, Ed. Keep talking."

"Well, I crashed the car into the wall and that stopped it. The airbag went off and that saved me from a lotta hurt, I think. No cars can park on that street because it's too steep, so that saved me, too, I guess. I didn't hit anybody else."

"Thank God for that – you could have done a lot worse on that steep hill. Are you okay?"

"Yeah, I'm okay. But later on they towed the car away – it's a pretty new Ford Escape and I haven't had any trouble with the brakes ever. The reason I'm telling you about this is they took the car to Ford's collision center over in White Bear

Lake. They called me from there today and said something was odd about the brake line to the front wheels. They said it looked 'worn.' That was the word they used, 'worn,' not cut, but worn, and the brake fluid had all drained out. I'm thinking that's odd, Otis, because that car is only two years old. I haven't run over anything or bumped it on the bottom or done anything else I can think of to damage the brake line. This shouldn't have happened and the whole thing just seems fishy to me. What do you think?"

"I think I want to look at your car, Ed. You got a rental to use?"

"Yes, I got one right away 'cuz I have to get to work."

"Meet me at the collision center as soon as you can get there. This does sound odd and I don't like it one bit. See you there," and Otis was on his way in minutes.

Both of them arrived at the center about the same time and talked with the mechanics. The technicians confirmed what Ed had told Otis, and they showed him the damaged brake line fitting. They found a tiny hole near the connection where the brake fluid leaked out, but it was impossible to tell if it had been deliberately damaged or not. The mechanics said it didn't look the way a two-year-old car should look, but they weren't able to firmly commit that it had been tampered with.

Just to be sure, Otis took the damaged brake line fitting with him. The collision center would only throw it away, and there was a chance, remote or not, that it could be evidence.

Back at Otis's office, the two of them talked about what might have happened. Crashing into the wall was the best resolution for the incident as the steepness of the hill could have involved other cars or even pedestrians and the possibilities were frightening. Ed was still a little shook up about the whole episode, and he was aching all over from the jolt of hitting the wall. Fortunately, the seatbelt had saved him from more serious injury. He was convinced that someone deliberately tried to sabotage his car. Otis was more objective about the matter, and because of the mechanic's hesitancy, he didn't have real proof the car was purposely impaired.

After discussing all the risks and options, they decided to keep careful watch on things and Ed left to go buy a new car as the other one was considered totaled. Otis agreed to continue to investigate what happened, and would certainly add the event to his growing list of oddities surrounding James Ward's death.

*****

A soft overnight rain perked up the flowers and the grass. Goldie had also perked up and McKenzie thought it might be time to take her along on her morning runs. A neighbor boy, Tyler, the younger son of the Iversons, had appeared at the door the day before. He said Judge Ward had been paying him to mow the lawn and did McKenzie want him to continue. She readily agreed and hired Tyler for the rest of the season.

She also expected to hear from whoever had been cleaning the house and made a note to ask Mary Jo about who it might be. She most definitely wanted that to continue and hoped Mary Jo knew who it was. McKenzie had been having daily phone calls with her about household things. Mary Jo was helping her to get reestablished in the town, and they were becoming good friends.

Dinner on Tuesday evening with William, Dolly, and Sophie, was unexpectedly good – at the beginning, at least. The

Lake Elmo Inn had been recently updated and the old dark woodwork gleamed beautifully. McKenzie remembered going there for special occasions with her family while she was growing up. Their signature salt and pepper shakers were on display as they had been for many years, and it still felt like a place to celebrate. She was wearing a simple blue Ralph Lauren sheath she brought with her from New York and wondered if this evening would be a celebration.

Dolly was right about the food still being great and McKenzie was pleased that the atmosphere was comfortable for all of them. Dolly looked beautiful in an ice-blue dress that accented her eyes. Sophia was a younger version of Dolly but her blond hair was longer and straighter as teens like to wear it. She was wearing white cutoffs and a brief top that showed much of her already-ample cleavage. Despite the warm summer weather, William was in a suit, which caused McKenzie a little surprise at his formality.

Conversation was stiff at first, considering the shock from the recent will-reading. McKenzie tried to diffuse the stiffness by asking Sophia about her school life and how it was growing up in Deep Lake. Dolly softened a little too, and they all chatted more easily. Sophia started talking about herself and her sports. She played tennis and McKenzie suggested a game with her soon, which caused some raised eyebrows from her parents.

"I thought you'd be leaving," William said, "in fact, I'm surprised you've stayed this long. You are selling the house, aren't you?"

McKenzie took a deep breath. "Things have changed, William. That's my big news. I've decided to stay in Deep Lake."

"What?!" gasped William and Dolly. At the same time, Sophia said, "That's great!"

"I expect it's a bit of a shock to you, but since I've been here I've learned that I miss the small-town environment. New York has lost its allure for me, and I'd like to try my hand at dealing with domestic real estate rather than commercial. On top of that, I'm not happy with the facts surrounding Dad's death. Otis and I are looking closer at some of the details about it."

"What sort of 'details?' I thought his death was determined to be of natural causes." William asked.

"Yes," agreed Dolly. "There are bees and wasps all over the place at this time of year. What's so unusual about that? It was just a terrible accident."

McKenzie didn't mean to spill the information about looking into her dad's death, but it just came out. She backpedaled, "Well yes, that's true, but I'm finding it hard to accept."

"We're all finding it hard to accept, McKenzie, but it happened and we have to deal with it," William declared. "So, are you staying on in the house?"

"Yes, I really like old houses, and this one is a fine example of sturdy architecture, not to mention all my memories there. I'll be checking into working with one of the local real estate companies while I settle in. I've started divesting myself of most of my New York business ventures, but that will take some time."

William huffed, "Hmmm. Well, good luck with getting rid of all the junk in the house. None of that stuff is of any interest to me."

Conversation got immediately taut again after McKenzie's news, and they began to wind up the evening. She made a tentative date with Sophia to play tennis in the next few days, and then the three of them drifted away.

"Well, that didn't go over well," McKenzie thought. "Too bad, William, I'm staying whether you like it or not."

*****

McKenzie drove home slowly through the countryside she was coming to like more and more. It wasn't quite dark yet, and her mind wandered through the many burdens she was carrying. Wandering mind or not, she remembered to keep an eye out for deer. They were plentiful in wooded areas especially in early morning and evening hours. Run-ins between cars and deer were more common than one would think.

There had been no more contact with Michael, and she didn't expect to hear from him again after their no-nonsense phone conversation the other day. A little wistful, she wondered what would happen or *if* something would happen with Ethan in the romance department. She was liking him more and more. While they were eating hamburgers and sitting in the yard swing earlier in the week she told him that she was staying in Deep Lake, and he almost choked.

"You are? Why that's great!" he exclaimed a little too loudly and then stammered. "I mean great for you and for your brother and his family, and ... well, for me, too, if you want to know. I really like you a lot, McKenzie, and I hope you'll keep seeing me."

"Yes, I will Ethan. I like being with you. I like your daughter, too, and I hope she likes me."

"You're all she talks about if you really want to know. You've made quite an impression on her already. In fact, now that things are changing and you are staying in Deep Lake, would you like to go with Isabella and me to Taylor's Falls this Saturday? It's a beautiful drive and they have a mini-golf course that's fun."

"I'd love to. It sounds like a good time."

They were picking her up about ten on Saturday and she was looking forward to the day with them. A day with Ethan and his little girl would be a good respite from wracking her brain over her father's death and working with Otis on trying to find out who almost ran her down with the pickup truck.

CHAPTER 18

WRESTLING WITH OPTIONS

McKenzie and Otis had spent some time going over the interviews with the neighbors and his chat with the old guys in front of the barbershop. McKenzie had been more attentive during her morning runs but hadn't seen anything that looked suspicious since the day of the truck incident.

A couple of mornings after her dinner with William's family, as she had breakfast after her morning's uneventful run, her niece Sophia unexpectedly called.

"Hi Aunt McKenzie, it's me, Sophie. I was like thinking about what you said about maybe playing a game of tennis with me. I literally don't have a thing planned to do today and both Mom and Dad are gone and I was like thinking maybe today might be a good time. It's gonna be hot later, but wanna try at least a set this morning?"

McKenzie was extremely pleased, as well as surprised, to hear from Sophie, and said, "I think that's a great idea, Sophie. I just went for my run this morning, but I think I can still hit a few balls. Where can I meet you?"

"Oh, that's awesome, Aunt McKenzie. I usually play at our club, but you're like not a member there, so how about we play at the public courts? They're not bad and they're close – over by the resort at the end of the lake. Like in an hour or so?"

"Sounds good to me – see you there."

McKenzie found some old tennis shorts and a tee shirt and dug out one of her high school tennis racquets. She didn't bring her good racquets with her from New York, and the ones she played with so many years before were sadly out of date. Tennis was a sport she had kept up with during her years in New York. Michael didn't share her enthusiasm for the game, so she always played at an indoor club with acquaintances she made there. In fact, that's where she met Desiree, her business partner, and they used to have some rousing doubles games with other friends from the club.

Sophie got to the courts first and was warming up by hitting balls against a backboard. She had her long hair in a ponytail that hung out the back of a trendy visor, and she was dressed in a classy one-piece tennis dress. It was white and she looked like she could be stepping on the courts at Wimbledon.

McKenzie felt a little tacky in her shorts and tee-shirt, but only for a moment. Sophie was happy to see her and they easily chatted about the coming game.

McKenzie won the coin toss and chose to receive instead of serve so she could see how well Sophie played. Sophie played extremely well and McKenzie didn't have to play down to her at all. In fact, with McKenzie's old racquet and Sophie's up-to-date Head Liquidmetal 8, the two of them were a good match. Sophie won the first game handily, 6-3, McKenzie the second, 6-4, and the third was a tie which McKenzie eventually won, 7-5. They decided to take a water break, and there was a comfortable bench in the shade where they admired each other's skills.

"You're really good, Aunt McKenzie, I'm like impressed – even with that old heavy racquet. I should'a brought one of my other racquets for you. The new ones are so much lighter."

"Thanks, Sophie, I do try to keep up with the game. Back in New York, I used to try to play once or twice a week, and I have some better racquets there, too. You're good yourself. How did you learn to play?"

"My mom sent me to a pro at our club. She wanted me to learn but she doesn't play at all. I played in high school, too, and was captain of our team in my senior year. It was kinda fun. Most of my friends play, but nobody was around today and that's when I thought I'd call you. I'm like glad I did."

McKenzie asked where her parents were that day, and Sophie answered, "Dad's at work and Mom went to see her brother."

"I didn't know your mom had a brother, Sophie. Where does he live?"

"Yeah, Uncle Tony lives in St. Paul with my grandma. I don't see them much, but Grandma came to my graduation. She almost didn't make it because Uncle Tony's old truck had a flat tire or something."

"Well, let's finish this set before it gets any hotter – looks like it's going to be a scorcher today," and they headed back to the court.

Sophie eventually won the set with her lighter racquet and younger body which hadn't already done a three-mile run that morning. They sat on the bench and chatted a little more about upcoming college for Sophie.

McKenzie asked, "Your mom said you might be interested in working at Ward Transport after college. What made you think about doing that?"

"My mom has always wanted me to work there because she said the company will belong to her and Dad. I like numbers, and it seems like it's literally the only thing she wants me to do. I remember going there to see Grandpa when I was little and that was fun. He took me around to see all the big trucks and I got to sit in one and that was really cool. I decided it might be fun to like work in a company that I might own someday."

McKenzie raised her eyebrows at Sophie's answer but decided to let it go. It was now late morning, and the day was heating up. McKenzie gave Sophie a hug. "Thanks for calling, this was fun. You were just a toddler when I left Deep Lake, and now you're already on your way to college. It's amazing how fast time goes. I'm sorry I missed all your growing up years, but I hope we can see more of each other now."

"So do I, Aunt McKenzie, you're much better than I expected. Bye," she said as she got into her car. It was a new bright blue Honda Civic, cute and smart, and was her graduation gift from her parents. She couldn't take it to college as she would be living on campus, but she told McKenzie it might be kept at Ward Transport in the new storage building until she needed it.

"So, I'm better than she expected, am I. I wonder what she expected," McKenzie mused as she headed home.

After a light lunch, resting with some iced tea and stroking Goldie at her side, she decided to stop in at Otis's office to see what more he might have found out. She didn't call, just headed over to his office.

"Well, hello there Kenzie. I was just thinking of you and was going to call. I've got some new information on Bobbie Winehauser and I'm ready to pay him a visit. Wanna come along?"

"I sure do. Anything I can do to help?"

"You've got good instincts and I'd appreciate another pair of eyes on his reaction when I question him. You don't have to say much, but your being there might bring it out if he's got something to hide."

"Let's go!"

The Winehauser farm was well on the way to Stillwater east of Deep Lake, and a couple of big dogs barked as they pulled into the driveway. It was a well-kept small acreage with several outbuildings, and the yard was neatly mowed around the old farmhouse. Two men who looked like father and son, came out of the house when they heard the barking to see who was arriving.

Otis got out of the car as they approached. "Mr. Winehauser? I'm Deputy Sheriff Otis Jorgensen."

"Yeah," said the older man, whose thin gray hair almost covered his scaly scalp. His small and watery eyes could have been brown, but the wrinkles around them were so deep his eyes were hardly visible. Both men were short and stocky, with massive arms. "I know who you are. Whadaya want here?"

"I'm just tying up some loose ends after the death of Judge Ward a couple of weeks ago. This is his daughter, McKenzie Ward."

The two men looked at McKenzie with such hatred, her face burned. Bobbie was wearing faded jeans and an equally faded tee shirt with an old sports logo. His small light brown eyes were more defined in his face, but were almost hidden under a ragged gray cap. Dull brown hair stuck out the sides and back of the cap. Both men had unshaven stubble on their chins, and were wearing heavy work boots. They looked like they had been working hard on something.

The elder Winehauser said, "Yeah, your dad made some bad calls when he was on the bench. One of them was sending my boy here to prison. He didn't have a very good lawyer, but he shouldn't have got such a stiff sentence for having a little weed on him."

Otis stepped closer to Winehauser and answered, "You know it was more than 'a little weed,' Mr. Winehauser. I've read up on Bobbie's case, and after a simple stop by a Stillwater traffic cop, almost a full pound of marijuana was found in his pickup. That's a lot more than could be considered 'recreational use' and qualifies as a felony. I think you should be glad his sentence wasn't longer."

Bobbie and his dad looked away. Otis continued, "We're not here to quibble about Bobbie's sentence, Mr. Winehauser. He's paid his dues and I hope he's on the straight and narrow now. We're looking for some information about a dirty gray pickup that's been sighted in town and could be up to no good. Either of you guys seen an older gray pickup around that doesn't seem on the up and up?"

Bobbie and his dad looked at each other and shrugged. Bobbie replied, "There's pickups all over this county, Deputy, you know that."

"What color is yours?" Otis asked.

"It's black, and settin' right over there, as you can see," the elder Winehauser said with a glare at Otis. "Bobbie's using it for work." He shifted his glare to McKenzie and said, "He's workin' over to Jack's tire shop in Hudson, and he's gotta get over there real soon."

McKenzie took a breath and dived in with the story she came up with on the way to the Winehauser farm. "We're asking around to see what local people around Deep Lake know about bees or wasps. Do you keep any, by chance or know of anyone around here who does?"

"Nah," Winehauser answered, "don't got any use for no bees. There's wasps around here now and again. Those bastards are nasty. I kill 'em any chance I get."

Otis took over and nodded at McKenzie. "It looks like you can't help us today, so we'll be off. Good luck to you Bobbie."

Gratefully, McKenzie got into the car with Otis. "Whew, I'm glad that's over," she said as they pulled out of the driveway. "But it's not over, to be honest. I didn't like the look of either of those men. Did you notice how Bobbie kept glancing back at the barn that was closest to the house? He looked at it several times while we were there, and I have to say the whole conversation just felt off, you know what I mean?"

"I saw it too, and I didn't like it either. It was good of you to notice the boy's glances. There's something that's not right about that place. I'll be watching it closer from here on."

*****

After the visit to the Winehausers, McKenzie decided to stop in to see Ed Johnson at Ward Transport. Things couldn't be too pleasant for him after the news of her father's will and her brother William's reaction. The lot looked busy with a couple of trucks loading or unloading goods from the big warehouse on the property. The warehouse looked new, McKenzie noted, as she didn't remember the building being there before. This must be where Sophie's car would be stored while she was away at college. There were a few cars in the lot that must have belonged to workers, but she didn't see William's car there.

Ed greeted her with a smile and a hug. "William told me the good news, McKenzie, that you're staying in Deep Lake. I hope you made the right decision. This for sure isn't New York, you know," and he chuckled.

"For sure, Ed, and that's why I'm staying. This town is in my blood and it didn't take long for me to realize I've been missing it. I wish it hadn't taken my dad's death to get me back here, but I'm here to stay."

"William isn't here this afternoon if you were hoping to see him," Ed said wistfully. "I have to say he hung around here more for a few days after the funeral, but the golf links had a wider appeal today, and he took off."

"I didn't come to see William, Ed. I have to say it's obvious that you're doing a good job of running this place. Tell me about the warehouse. Is it new?"

Ed was clearly pleased to see McKenzie's interest in the company, and he gave her a tour of the whole facility, which had changed a lot since she left sixteen years before. Now there were a half-dozen company drivers and at least as many contractors doing less-than-truckload deliveries in and around the Twin Cities. The warehouse worked to combine shipments and had been a money-maker as well as a convenience. Two dispatchers gave her a nod as she walked through the main office with Ed, and both were busy on their phones with customers. The office manager, Patty Thomas, had come to work for McKenzie's grandfather, Big Jim Ward, right out of high school. She was now sixty-two and had no visions of retiring soon. He introduced McKenzie, and Patty remembered her as a girl. She was pleased to see she was showing some attention to the company. Patty told McKenzie she had high regard for her father, but didn't say anything about William.

Ed said he couldn't live without her, and Patty gave him a no-nonsense smirk.

"I could use a cup of coffee and a chat, if you've got the time, Ed," McKenzie said after the tour.

They each got a fresh cup from the pot in the break room. Ed ushered her into a comfortable but economically furnished office. They sat, and McKenzie looked at him with a sigh. "Ed, I've decided to confide in you and I hope you're not shocked by what I have to say."

"Thank you, I appreciate your confidence, but I have to say I'm not shocked easily. What's up?"

"I've been working with Deputy Sheriff Otis Jorgensen on my father's death. I think you need to know that we believe this was not an accident. Somehow, someone introduced those wasps to where my father was. Someone who knew about his severe allergy and what the consequences would be."

"Oh McKenzie, that's serious! Are you sure about that?"

"As sure as anyone can be. Ethan Thompson, the vet, knows about bee and wasp behavior, and he and Otis have been searching for nests in the area where Dad was going to fish. They haven't found a single possibility that so many wasps would have been in one place to sting him so many times. They both believe there is foul play involved here, and we are trying privately to work out who might have done this and how it happened."

"This is hard to take in. James was so highly regarded, and I have to say he was very open about his allergy. Almost anyone who knew him at all was aware of it, I believe."

"There's more, Ed, and this might be even harder to take in. I was very nearly deliberately run over a few days ago. I was out for my morning run, which I'm afraid is already an established routine to anyone who has a reason to take notice of it. I believe someone has been watching me and knew when I would be at that particular intersection."

"This is getting scary, McKenzie."

"You bet it is. From my brief look at the vehicle, I think it was a gray pickup with a lot of dirt on it. One of my neighbors saw such a pickup in our neighborhood, and it sounds like someone has been watching me, plus I've also had a middle-of-the-night phone call that was threatening."

"Gray pickups would be plentiful in our neck of the woods. I'm afraid I can't help you there, but this is really frightening. I don't know if Otis told you that I had a strange thing happen the other day with the brakes on my car. The mechanical inspection turned out to be inconclusive, but I'm still confused about what happened. It just didn't feel right, you know what I mean?" He then told her the details of losing the brakes and hitting the courthouse wall.

McKenzie scowled and said, "I don't like this either, Ed. We've got to find out what is going on here and who is responsible for it."

Johnson asked, "How do you think I could help?"

"Do you know of any disgruntled drivers or customers or anyone else associated with the trucking company who might have held a grudge against my father?" McKenzie asked with more than a little desperation.

"I'm wracking my brain here. You know, we had a former driver a while ago who was let go when we discovered he was stealing from loads and falsifying logs. He had a girlfriend in

Minneapolis and would spend his afternoons with her and cheat on his hours. We had to let him go, and I know he wasn't happy about it. I talked with James about it because we were wondering if the guy was doing other stuff that we should have him arrested for. We decided to just fire him and let it go at that because we didn't have enough proof even though I knew he was stealing from loads. The guy knew that James was involved in the firing and may have had enough of a grudge against him to do something. I don't know."

"If you can give me his name, I'll have Otis check him out," McKenzie said. "I might even pay him a visit myself."

"Now that I'm remembering, we've had some incidents with union organizers. We've always been a non-union company and our employees have been happy with their jobs and the benefits. I know Ward Transport has been targeted for union organizing several times through the years, and we've been able to hold them off for quite a while.

Most of the union guys have been professional about their contacts, but I heard we had a couple of really nasty guys show up and park their cars just off our property. They would taunt our drivers and say things like, 'Have you seen your wife today? I have,' and it scared the bejesus out of them. James came over then and talked with the men. I don't know what he said, but they left and we didn't see them again, but they were definitely not happy. James told us he had taken care of things for now, but he wasn't happy about it either. He told William and me to keep a close watch on the property and call him if anything like that happened again. This was about six months ago and we didn't have any more trouble that I'm aware of. I've been thinking since then about getting a dog to patrol the property at night, but I haven't done anything about it yet. Just procrastinating, I guess. You know how it goes."

"Unfortunately, I do. I think people relax in a small town – and you believe bad things can't happen like they do in big cities. I'm learning they happen everywhere. It makes me more determined than ever to find out what happened to my father, besides what's going on with me. I'm pissed if you really want to know, Ed," she said with a grim chortle.

"I can tell, McKenzie, and I don't blame you. Now that you're spelling it all out for me, I can see something's not right. I'll do some digging to get the names of the union guys who were harassing my drivers and the guy we had to fire, and let you know what I find."

Thanks, Ed. I'd appreciate it if you didn't tell anyone else about what we're looking at. We were able to bury my father, but the circumstances of his death are far from settled. We're holding this close for now and appreciate your good judgment in looking at anything that might be suspicious. As far as getting a patrol dog, that's a good idea. Ethan Thompson could help you find just the right one, I have no doubt."

"I'll do that. Thank you so much for trusting me with this information. You know I'll help however I can. Your dad was one of the finest men I ever knew and we need to get to the bottom of what's going on."

"Goodbye for now, Ed. We'll be talking again soon."

"Goodbye, McKenzie. I'm glad you're staying and it goes without saying that you're welcome to stop in here whenever you want to."

McKenzie sat a moment in her car before driving away. She decided to go home and start the process of becoming a real estate agent for her new area. She realized it was a great way to sleuth and nose around properties to check out anything that looked suspicious. She didn't need to make a lot of money because of funds supplied by her New York holdings and only needed to work enough to keep her hand in the business and follow her instincts. She was determined to find her father's killer. There was that word again. Killer. She hated to even think it, but it was time to call a spade a spade. Determination coursed through her body and she headed home to make lists of what needed to be done. Getting her real estate license was at the top for now.

CHAPTER 19
SIX WEEKS LATER

Six weeks had gone by and McKenzie was settling into life in Deep Lake. It was now the end of August, and she had completed the extensive training she needed to become a residential real estate agent in Minnesota. The instructors were impressed with her New York education and experience, but rules are rules, and she had to take the full course. She had to work with another broker for two years before becoming a broker herself, and she had already chosen a broker to work with and joined the Saint Paul Area Association of Realtors as well as the Minnesota Association of Realtors and the National Association of Realtors. She chose to join Minnesota's Best Real Estate and had signed a contract with them only the day before.

"Here I go again," McKenzie thought. "This is going to be another whole new adventure." She had always loved houses, especially the older ones. This could be fun and she was eager to get going. She had to get signs made, and the most work would be in finding properties to list. Time for another visit to Janice and Vicky? That could be the perfect way to get the word out. There would be press releases and the like, but letting the girls spread the word through their customers would help, too.

She had mostly put her unofficial investigation of her father's murder on hold to get her real estate license. She believed her job as a realtor would help gain easier access to properties – and people – who might be able to shed information on what happened.

Otis was still looking at possibilities, but he hadn't come up with anything concrete, and other issues in the town had taken more of his time.

Several weeks after the discussion with Ed Johnson, she and Otis met with one of the Teamster union organizers. In his downtown Minneapolis office, tall and handsome Teamster leader David Cross was smooth and polished and dressed in an impeccable navy-blue suit. When they told him about the actions of the individuals harassing company drivers, he adamantly denied that any of his organizers would behave as Johnson had described. He did admit that Ward Transport had been a target for Teamster organization. However, Cross eventually told them they had decided to back off trying to unionize the company because they didn't want to deal with a business owned by a judge.

McKenzie believed Ed Johnson's description of the union guys' actions. Did one of them find out about the judge's allergy and decide to eliminate that problem? Cross didn't give the names of the men who were on Ward Transport's property, but she decided to look a little further into this.

Back at home after their unsuccessful trip to see David Cross, McKenzie decided to do something on her own. She reverted to her NYC persona of fearless bravura, and after a little searching on Google, made a phone call to Cross's office. She had noticed that calls were forwarded through a receptionist while she and Otis were waiting at the office, and the receptionist was young and friendly. She had long reddish hair that she continued to flip out of her heavily made-up eyes, and a blouse with several buttons undone, along with a dimpled smile that invited glances at her peek-a-boo cleavage. Deciding the girl could be easily intimidated, McKenzie used the name of a woman connected with the Teamster Union's major office whom she found on Google, and called the office.

After answering the phone pleasantly, the receptionist said, "How may I help you?"

Stern and tough, McKenzie said, "This is Alice Rossi from Teamster headquarters in Detroit. I understand there have been some inquiries about that Ward Transport company out there. Exactly who were the goons who approached the company six months ago?"

"Well, that would be in Mr. Cross's responsibility. Do you want me to put you through to him?"

"No, I just want to know who went out there. You know those guys and you can give that to me," McKenzie said with authority.

Duly intimidated, she girl answered, "We've got a few guys who like to hassle people sometimes and Mr. Cross gets really upset about it, Ms. Rossi, but I think it was Dario Esposito and Frank De Angelis. Are you sure you don't want to talk with Mr. Cross?"

"No, that'll do," and she hung up abruptly.

"Yes!" McKenzie shouted loud enough to rouse a sleeping Goldie. "With a little help from Google, I'll find those guys, and maybe we'll get somewhere," she said to herself.

CHAPTER 20
LOVE AMID ANXIETY

McKenzie had gone to the mini-golf course in Taylor's Falls with Ethan and his daughter several weeks before and had had a great afternoon. She hadn't played mini-golf since high school and remembered the place as a date spot for kids. It still seemed to be, but she was surprised at how much fun it was – all around fun like she hadn't had for a long time. Too long.

The drive-in restaurant in town had to be one of the last of its kind, but the hamburgers were good and the root beer floats divine. The three of them sat where a beautiful fountain splattered a few drops of cool water on them now and then. It felt wonderful on a hot day. Isabella made the day brighter than the sparkling July sun and her laughter was a joy to hear. During the game, McKenzie missed putting her ball through the underground passageway several times and she and Isabella had a good laugh at her ineptitude.

The three of them had gone out to eat or stayed at McKenzie's house to play games several times over the past weeks. They also went fishing one day at the shallow end of Deep Lake. They rented a boat from the resort and had a great day on the water. McKenzie packed a picnic lunch and they ate their sandwiches on a blanket at the water's edge. Between them they caught several small sunfish and one nice bass. McKenzie was surprised that Isabella could bait her own hook

– they were using worms as bait. It was obvious that Ethan had taught his daughter to fish when she was really young, and her confidence was delightful to see.

Ethan cleaned the bigger fish and with Isabella's help, McKenzie cooked it for their dinner at her house later. The day brought many memories of fishing with her father, of course, and filled her with nostalgia.

McKenzie had also gone to dinner alone with Ethan a number of times, and they were becoming more and more comfortable with each other. No longer needing the excuse to see how Goldie was healing, Ethan called her at odd hours to just say "Hi," and McKenzie brightened each time she heard his voice. Late night partings were getting more difficult, and McKenzie was reluctant to slow down the pace of their quickly developing relationship. Things were moving faster than they probably should, she told herself, but they had both experienced loss and thought they knew what they were doing. Why not just enjoy their emerging relationship and see where it might lead?

Interrupting her thoughts as she sat with coffee to plan her day, her cell phone rang with the special ring she had programmed for Ethan.

"Hey, Kenzie," as he had taken to calling her, "how about dinner tonight on the St. Croix?"

"On the St. Croix … you mean on a raft, or did you bite the bullet and buy a boat?" she quipped.

"I mean on one of the big boats – the River Star. I've got tickets for a dinner cruise." The River Star was one of several big riverboats that offered lunch and dinner cruises on the Saint Croix River which divided Minnesota and Wisconsin. The bluffs on either side of the river were gorgeous through all seasons and the boats, several stories high and equipped with old-fashioned paddle wheels, provided lovely several-hour trips.

"Now that sounds great. What about Isabella – will she go along?"

"No, Isabella's spending the night with Jane in Edina, so there's no rush," he said with a hopeful tone. Jane Rostad was Ethan's deceased wife's mother. Jane was a widow whose husband died young of a cancer similar to that which took their daughter, Elizabeth. An attractive widow not yet sixty, Jane preferred to stay single and worked part-time at an expensive dress shop in the Galleria, an upscale shopping center not far from her home. McKenzie had met her a couple of times and Jane was friendly toward her, albeit a little surprised that Ethan seemed so interested in McKenzie. When his wife died five years before, Ethan was so lost and devastated, he didn't date for several years, as he had told McKenzie. After that, he was cautious about dating and did so seldom. When he met McKenzie, everything seemed to speed up and McKenzie had noticed that Jane began to take more notice of this new woman in her son-in-law's life.

They made plans for Ethan to pick her up that evening and McKenzie was eagerly looking forward to their date.

*****

McKenzie had Googled the two "goons" whose names she got from the receptionist at the Teamsters' office. She had addresses and decided to check them out herself before saying anything to Otis. She drove to St. Paul, which called itself "the most livable city in America." There were dozens of beautiful quiet neighborhoods throughout the city, which certainly helped the city live up to its hype, but some areas were not so beautifully "livable." Dario Esposito lived in Frogtown, an area that surrounded University Avenue just west of downtown St. Paul. There was a high concentration of crime in that area around Western Avenue, Dale Street, and Victoria Avenue.

Frogtown dated back to the 1860s and '70s. It was called Froschenberg in German, or Frogtown because of the many swamps and wetlands, and every evening was filled with the sounds of croaking frogs. Houses there had nearly always been owned or rented by immigrant factory workers and tradesmen. The houses were built tall and narrow, some on twenty-five-foot lots. It was said when you wanted to meet your neighbors, you just had to stick your hand out the window and shake hands with the guy next door who was doing the same thing.

McKenzie found the address for Esposito, parked and made her way up the cracked cement walk. She took a deep breath and knocked on the door of a questionably-maintained three-story narrow house that most likely was one of the originals in the neighborhood. After several minutes, a woman came to the door.

The woman was rough, with thick and unruly brown/gray hair, faded brown eyes, and thin lips that turned down at the edges, almost like a cartoon. She wasn't heavy, but had a square body and she was wearing an old-fashioned house dress of a bleached-out unidentifiable print. Her skinny legs seemed to just hang out the bottom of the dress and ended in heavy boots with thick soles.

McKenzie felt like she had gone back in time, as she asked, "Is Mr. Esposito home?"

"Nah, he ain't here. He's workin' today and that's a good thing. Who are you and why you askin'? "

"I'm McKenzie Ward," using her real name, "I'm a real estate agent, and we're interested in some of the older homes in this area."

"Don't know why – this place is a dump, but the rent is cheap," the woman sneered.

"I would be interested in speaking with Mr. Esposito, briefly, anyway. Are you Mrs. Esposito?"

"Yes, that's m'name – I'm Dario's mother. The other Mrs. Esposito, his wife, cut out a couple a years ago, the lazy broad. Took the kids and just disappeared. Said she couldn't stand it anymore, whatever 'it' was."

"Oh, I'm sorry. Can you tell me where or when I might be able to speak with him – about his experience with houses in this area?"

"He might be home later tonight, otherwise he usually goes to Davey's Bar over on Dale to hoist a few. A few too many, the way I sees it."

"Well, thank you for your time," McKenzie said and walked quickly back down the sidewalk.

She got in her car and immediately locked the doors. "Whew," she thought, "what am I getting myself into?"

McKenzie drove home via a detour down Dale Street and went by Davey's Bar. She was weighing in her mind whether she had the courage or just plain guts, to confront Esposito at the bar. Should she go alone, or should she first talk about it with Otis? He might think she was crazy, but she had to know. Somehow, she felt by surprising Esposito and getting him off guard, she would know if this was the man who either arranged the killing or actually murdered her father.

It had already been more than two months since her father died. Otis was working on other leads, and she believed she could share whatever information she found out from Esposito with Otis later without bothering him now. That night was her big date with Ethan. She decided to confront Esposito later in the week at the bar his mother mentioned. She didn't know yet whether she would go alone, or not.

CHAPTER 21
JOY AND ANGST

E than and McKenzie were sitting by the railing on the top deck of the River Star and loving every moment of their dinner cruise. The late August evening was warm but the river breezes were cooling and the ever-present pesky Midwest mosquitoes were back on shore. The air smelled faintly of flowers and of the lemony dessert they had just eaten, along with the clean smell of water as it was churned up by the paddle wheel on the huge boat. It was a gorgeous evening. They had gone under the new bridge linking Minnesota and Wisconsin and down past Hudson and Afton before heading back to Stillwater. There were smaller boats buzzing around them, some with water skiers in tow, trying to catch the last of the daylight, and a few small sailboats were still out, too, with jaunty sails catching the wind. The setting sun sparkled on gentle waves in the river.

Ethan was stroking her hand and his fingers were gentle and light. The two of them were becoming so comfortable in each other's presence they no longer needed to make meaningless conversation and had been quiet for a time. He now said, "We're almost docked already, but I don't want the evening to end. How about you?"

"Hmm, let's go back to my house, Ethan, I don't want it to end either."

He knew exactly what she was proposing, and anticipation built for both of them. Disembarking the boat and getting out of the beautiful but crowded river town of Stillwater took time, and they were both a little anxious about what was to come. Finally, they got to McKenzie's house and she told him to park in the alley behind her garage. They both knew he wouldn't be leaving early that night.

Goldie greeted them sleepily and after a few pats, she settled in her kitchen bed. Ethan put his arms around McKenzie and kissed her deeply. They leaned into each other with passion rising. Finally, leaning back with a deep breath, he said, "Are you nervous, too?"

"I was, but not anymore. I've fallen in love with you Ethan Thompson. This feels right and I don't want to wait any longer."

He was ecstatic to hear her declaration, held her closer and deepened their kiss. Looking intensely into her bottomless blue eyes while holding her tightly, he said thickly, "I've been waiting to hear you say that. I've loved you from the first week we met, but I was scared to say it until I knew you felt the same. You've become part of my heart."

They quietly went upstairs to her room. They were both a little embarrassed when they looked at the waiting bed, but embarrassment turned to need as their kisses intensified. Soon their clothing was shed and the thrill of feeling skin on skin was overwhelming. They fell together on the bed with arms and legs braided together as passion ruled.

*****

The next morning, McKenzie woke slowly and languished with a delicious smile on her face. She reached over to the empty spot on the bed and wished Ethan was still there. He most reluctantly left some time before dawn, but she grabbed the pillow and inhaled his lingering scent. She was filled with feelings of wonder about their love-making and realized she had never felt this way before. It wasn't just sex, it was truly making love between the two of them.

Her thoughts were interrupted by her ringing phone. It was an urgent ring, she believed, and instantly thought how silly that sounded – how could a telephone ring sound urgent?

She stilled it. "Hello?"

It was Otis, and he did sound urgent. "Kenzie, something has happened and we need to talk. Can you come down to my office this morning?"

"Of course I can – give me forty-five and I'll be there."

"You don't need to rush, but I think you'll be interested in what's been going on."

McKenzie put Goldie out by herself and true to her word, she was in Otis's office within forty-five minutes.

There was a strange man with Otis. He was a strong-looking man in his late forties or so, with graying sandy-colored hair, and what looked like a permanent scowl on his face. He examined McKenzie with light gray-brown eyes the same color as his hair. He was wearing a rumpled suit that looked like it needed a cleaning.

Otis introduced him simply as John Hart. Hart shook her hand and said he was happy to meet her.

Otis started, "Remember how we were both uncomfortable about the Winehauser farm when we went to check out Bobbie and his dad about the gray pickup?"

"Yes, there was something about how Bobbie kept looking at the big barn near the house. He looked nervous and I just didn't feel good about the whole conversation."

"You were right. As soon as I got back to my office that day, I called the sheriff and we worked together to set some plain-clothesmen on a watch detail because something didn't look right to me either. It took a few weeks, but we caught 'em."

"Caught who, Otis? Are you telling me you caught my father's killer?"

"Unfortunately not, Kenzie. I don't think the Winehausers had anything to do with your dad's death, but thanks partly to your good instincts, we caught another big fish and some smaller ones, too. It turns out that Bob Winehauser, Bobbie's father, has a brother up north near Baudette, by the Canadian border. This brother has a farm that is really remote – I mean it's waaay back in the boondocks. We began to notice that Bobbie was making trips up north with his father's bigger truck, and he was going more often than just to visit his uncle. Our plain-clothesmen followed him one day and found this uncle was growing marijuana in huge plots on the edges of the other crops on his farm. Bobbie was transporting the pot from the uncle's farm to the big barn on the Winehauser farm. He'd come back at night to unload. In fact, the barn we were curious about was full of it, buried under hay that was supposed to be hiding it. Bobbie was delivering small amounts of weed at a time to local dealers. The tire shop where he's been supposedly working was a hub for moving most of the marijuana around the country.

Marijuana is legal in Minnesota for medical purposes, but not in Wisconsin, at least for now. This cache was definitely not for medical purposes, and we stopped a growing organization of illegal marijuana distribution. Both Bobbie and his father won't be getting out of prison soon, and we collared the uncle and several others along the line, too. Jack's tire shop is out of business for good, and Jack himself had drug contacts all over the country and beyond. The Feds even got involved in the case because of multiple states being included in the whole sticky situation."

"Wow, you mean you've been working on this since the day we went out to Winehauser's farm six weeks ago?"

"I have. I'm sorry I couldn't talk with you about it while this was all going down, but things have been a little crazy here for the past month or so. John here, is with the FBI. He's been a great help in pulling all this together and we couldn't have done it without him.

"I wanted you to meet John because I took the liberty of telling him a little about our dilemma with your dad's death. Of course, he can't do anything about it and it's really not fair to involve the FBI on a local case, but hey, when he and I were sharing a brew after all the Winehauser events came together, I have to say that we talked a little about your dad's case."

McKenzie's eyes widened and she quickly drew in a breath. "You did?"

"We did, Miss Ward," Hart said, in a deep but sincere voice. "I wish I could stay to help, but I'm leaving in minutes for another multiple state drug case, and I've got to do my job. However, I agree with Otis that you've got a big problem in finding out who killed your father. The theory about transporting the wasps may sound crazy, but I think there might be some truth in it.

"I've urged Otis to keep looking at people Judge Ward might have offended on the bench, and there's that guy who was fired from the trucking company. Unfortunately, your deputy sheriff has been a little busy with drug lords the past few weeks to do any digging on your case, but I expect now he'll get back at it. Please don't be offended, Miss Ward, but I've told Otis he should be looking at people who might not have an obvious motive or criminal background, and that includes people like your brother."

"William?" McKenzie gasped.

"Yes, even William." Otis agreed. "He's not the only one, but we can't discount him without checking things out. John has given me a few tips on how to go about the search, and the sheriff agrees and supports me. I hope you understand."

McKenzie was rocked. She realized she had been reluctant to suspect her brother, but she did understand, and she wanted to put all of this to rest as soon as it could be done. She said, "This hurts, Otis, as I'm sure you know, but we need to find out what happened and why. I do understand, and I will help you any way I can.

"Agent Hart, thank you for coming here to work with Otis in closing down what must have been a wide-spread drug ring. I don't like to think of this sort of thing happening in my small town, but I know it happens everywhere. Thank you too, for talking with Otis about my father's death. We're going to solve this, there is no doubt."

Agent Hart shook hands with McKenzie and Otis, and as he headed out the door, said not goodbye, but "Godspeed." And he was gone.

CHAPTER 22

CONFRONTING DANGER

McKenzie was exhausted, mentally and physically from the day's events, and headed home for some peace. Peace was what she had found in her parents' old house. She wrapped herself in the house's sounds and the smells of old wood and real plastered walls, infused with the ups and downs of life as it had been lived by the people who had sheltered here for more than 150 years. As much as the day's activities had shaken her, she dug her hands in Goldie's warm fur and began to unwind. Feeling the dog's big heart beat against her palm, she thought over what she had learned that day and rethought her plan to confront Esposito. She had planned to go to Davey's Bar to check him out that evening, but her common sense prevailed.

While McKenzie was thinking over the events of the day, Ethan called. She sighed in anticipation of his voice. "Hi, Kenzie. I miss you, and I can't stop thinking about last night. I've been worthless at the clinic today because all I can think about is you. I called Mrs. Ambercrombie's dog by the wrong name this morning and Ginny looked at me like I was nuts. Are you okay?"

"I'm better than okay. I loved last night and I miss you, too. I'm a little distracted, though, and have lots to talk about. What are your plans tonight?"

"I'm picking up Isabella after work, but I can stop at your house for a few minutes on my way to Edina. I'll probably have to stay for a quick supper with Isabella and Jane. I'd rather be with you, but fatherhood calls. Does that work for you?"

"It does. We'll have more alone-time together soon. But I've got other news for you, too. Seeing you for even a few minutes is better than nothing. See you about five?"

"You got it. I love you and I want to shout it from the rooftops," Ethan said softly as he hung up.

*****

McKenzie hadn't had the chance to tell Otis anything about Esposito when she was at his office that day and she was curious enough to want to still check him out. She decided to call Janice and maybe the two of them could make the trip to the bar on Dale Street later that night as long as Ethan was busy. McKenzie had confided in Janice about the mystery surrounding her father's death. She hadn't given her any details, but it was enough for her to know that it wasn't settled and foul play was suspected.

Janice picked up the call when Vicky told her it was McKenzie, "Hello you, been wondering what's happening."

"My world is spinning, girl, and there's lots to tell. But first, I need some help. You busy tonight?" McKenzie asked.

"My TV shows can wait, what'cha got in mind – something fun?"

"Well, I don't know about fun, exactly. I want to check out somebody at Davey's Bar over on Dale Street, and I don't want to go alone. Wanna go sleuthing with me?"

"How can I resist – hmm, Davey's Bar on Dale – sounds like you do need somebody with you. That's a kinda rough neighborhood. Got a new boyfriend?"

"I wouldn't call him a boyfriend – more like a suspect. How does that sound?"

Janice perked up, "Now that does sound like fun!"

They agreed for McKenzie to pick Janice up about eight and for both of them to dress a little 'sleazy' so they'd fit in with the crowd, according to Janice.

*****

Just after five, Ethan rapped on the door and the moment they saw each other, they were wrapped so tightly, they seemed as one. "Oh, Kenzie, I know it's a stupid cliché, but how have I lived so long without you?" He took a deep breath and inhaled her unique and tantalizing fragrance and kissed her again.

McKenzie also took a deep breath, and said, "Hello to you, too, Ethan," while both of them broke into laughter.

They sat in the kitchen and McKenzie told him of developments from the day before and the visit with the FBI agent. Ethan admired her great instincts in telling Otis of her suspicions about the barn at the Winehauser place. He knew it was by her suggestion that Otis followed up on his own niggling misgivings about the place and delved deeper into the case. McKenzie told Ethan that unfortunately, it was ultimately determined that neither of the Winehausers had anything to do with her father's death.

Ethan was a little nervous when she told him she was going with Otis to check out the fired truck driver soon, but he had faith that Otis would watch out for her and agreed it was the right thing to do. Because of Ethan's concern about her going with Otis to confront the truck driver, McKenzie decided not to tell him about her plans for that evening. She knew he would strongly object, and she felt compelled to go through with the plans she had made with Janice. She did, however, mention the FBI agent had suggested looking more closely into her brother's actions and that they needed to clear him of any suspicion in their father's death. This was terribly hard for her to accept and she cried a little as she and Ethan talked about it. No matter what William had or had not done, he was her brother.

"I know this upsets you but I can't imagine that William had anything to do with this. Of course, Otis needs to talk seriously with him to clear up any doubt. We need to find out what happened to James to ease everyone's minds," Ethan said as he held her hands.

His calming nature encouraged her to relax a little. Neither of them wanted their short time together to end, but he continued, "Traffic will be bad at this time of day and I need to get way across town, so I'd better be on my way."

They stood and held each other tenderly while their thoughts went in a myriad of directions. "Please take care of yourself, my darling. Now that we've found each other we can't let anything happen to break us apart."

McKenzie felt a rush of warmth at his words and nodded into his neck as he held her. "I'll be fine, my sweet Ethan. Now you'd better be on your way or Isabella will think you deserted her. Give her my love and we'll talk more tomorrow." Several kisses later, she shoved him out the door with a sigh and a silent prayer that everything really would be fine.

*****

At eight o'clock on the dot, McKenzie pulled up to Janice's house. She was dressed in her blue Capri outfit and sandals, about as "sleazy" as she could think of. Janice floated out the door in a brightly printed short sundress that showed lots of cleavage. Her hair was wild and abundant, and sparkly sandals laced up to her knees. McKenzie leaned over to open the car door for Janice and said, "Now *that's* sleazy – don't know if I measure up."

With a chuckle, Janice quipped, "You'll do, girl – just put some red lipstick on and you're good – here's mine," and she handed over the lipstick.

McKenzie pulled down the mirror and applied the garish color, saying, "Now I look like a clown."

"It'll just add to the circus where we're goin' honey. This is gonna be fun!" And off they went to Davey's Bar.

The parking lot was almost filled with pickups and some older cars. It was most definitely a man's bar, but here and there were feminine personalized licenses that said things like, "PRINCESS," or "CUPC8C." Inside the bar it took a few minutes for their eyes to adjust to the darkness. It was late summer now, but still fairly light outside and the bar's "mood lighting" was just plain gloomy. A bright light spread out over the pool table and several men were gathered around it. When McKenzie and Janice entered, everyone in the club turned to look at them. Janice led the way to two stools at the bar amid several low whistling sounds they could still hear over the clacking of pool balls. McKenzie followed and mentally slid into her New York no-nonsense persona.

"What'll it be ladies," the bartender asked.

McKenzie asked for a glass of red wine and Janice opted for rum and coke on ice. After getting their drinks, they sat there at the bar a while and looked around the large room. A number of tables were occupied by small groups of people laughing and chatting and enjoying their drinks. A group of serious pool players hovered under the center light over the table and rubbed chalk on their pool cues while they waited their turn. McKenzie wondered if Esposito was one of the men around the pool table. A few minutes later, Janice spied an open table, and they headed over to it and took seats.

"What now," McKenzie thought, and before the thought was out of her mind, a man was standing by her side.

"So, are you gals slummin' or what? Haven't seen you in here before. I'm Colton and I'm happy to see you," said the stocky, swarthy, and over-confident looking man leaning on their table.

"Hi," said McKenzie, "We're from Stillwater," thinking she'd rather not say where they really lived.

Colton slid into the chair next to McKenzie and clinked his glass to hers. "Well, I'm glad you finally found your way to where you're s'posed to be, Sweetie."

Suddenly, a loud crash behind their table briefly caught everyone's attention.

She and Janice turned suddenly to see that another man who looked much like Colton, had dropped a beer glass. The glass was fairly empty, but beer and glass had shattered and splashed on the hard tile floor, just missing the girls. In the instant, while their attention was behind them, the man called Colton slipped something into each of their drinks.

"Sorry about that, girls, my friend Trey here is a good guy, but he's a total klutz. He'll get us all another round as an apology, right Trey," Colton said without a question, as he grinned at McKenzie, clinked his glass against hers again, and said, "Cheers."

Janice and McKenzie raised eyebrows at each other and sipped their drinks.

Trey himself swept up the mess behind them, and he returned momentarily with more drinks. The girls kept their original drinks, setting the new ones aside. Introducing themselves all around, Colton said, "So, what brings you to this part of town?"

Janice started by saying, "McKenzie here is in real estate. She's interested in the old houses in Frogtown."

"I don't know what could be interesting about those old houses," Trey said, "Let's talk about you, instead, Janice. You've got the most gorgeous head of hair I ever saw. And the rest of you goes right with it. Drink up, and let's have a dance." Within a few minutes, Janice and Trey headed off to choose some songs to dance to.

Colton continued to hit on McKenzie, and he added, "My friend Dario lives in one of those old houses in Frogtown. He's playing pool now, but maybe we'll call him over later to see if he can help you with what you want to know about them."

McKenzie was thrilled to hear Colton mention Dario. After all, that's why she was there and what a stroke of luck to find somebody right away who knew him. She had finished her glass of wine, and suddenly realized she felt odd. Not just odd, but really good, euphoric, in fact, and caught herself giggling at something Colton had said. Abruptly, she realized she shouldn't be feeling so good ... something was wrong. She stood, rather unsteadily she recognized, and stumbled to the ladies' room. Not giving herself a chance to consider the alternatives, she pulled out her cell phone and quickly called Otis on her speed dial, while she could still do it. She said only, "Help us, Davey's Bar." She then went back to the barroom and grabbed Janice's shoulder. Janice had been dancing up a storm, enjoying herself immensely with Trey, and pulled away from McKenzie.

"Janice, we have to leave. Something's not right."

Janice frowned and started to argue that she was having a great time and why did they have to leave now. McKenzie pulled Janice with her and they staggered back to the ladies' room and locked the door. "Something's wrong here – I think they put something in our drinks. I called Otis and he's coming to get us. We're in trouble."

The two of them huddled in the restroom, feeling stupid and off-center. They wanted to go back and keep having fun – the music sounded so good and by that time they'd both forgotten why they were there in the first place. They were leaning against the wall and then slid to the floor holding each other's hands and began to study their fingernails intensely.

Suddenly, the restroom door crashed open. Otis was there in full uniform with his gun in his hand. He put the gun away and grabbed them both, hauling them out of the restroom, through the bar and out the door. The crowd had hastily thinned right after Otis yanked open the street door and queried the bartender. Otis knew he wouldn't have any luck finding the guilty parties that night because most of the people were already gone. Knowing time was critical because date-rape-drugs can dissipate quickly, he dragged both McKenzie and Janice stumbling and tripping out to his squad car.

He stopped at St. John's Hospital in Maplewood on the way back to Deep Lake. In the ER, both women were given urine tests which confirmed the presence of Rohypnol. It happened that Otis had recently had some new information cross his desk about date-rape drugs and how their use was spreading. Rohypnol was believed to be commonly used in drug facilitated sexual assault – known as DFSA – in the United States and other countries. The drug was also known as Roofies, Ruffies, Mind Erasers, Trip-and-Fall, and more. Rohypnols came as a pill that dissolved in liquids and could be used to treat depression caused by other drugs. They were not legally manufactured in the U.S., but stolen from foreign pharmaceutical companies and had been sold all over the U.S. since the 1990s.

Originally colorless, when slipped into a drink, a dye in the newer pills made clear liquids turn bright blue and dark drinks turn cloudy, but the color change would have been hard to see in a dark drink, like cola or dark beer, or in a dark room. Unfortunately, both girls had dark-colored drinks that hid the dye. Later, McKenzie remembered she had thought her wine tasted odd, but she thought this was because it was a cheap brand.

Leaving the hospital, Otis delivered Janice to her mother's care and took McKenzie home with him for Mary Jo to tuck in bed in their guest room. He would deal with the men in the bar the next day as they had already left by the back door when he arrived at Davey's, and the bartender feigned ignorance of the whole incident. Sighing in relief that the girls had not been assaulted further, he and Mary Jo sat at the kitchen table and talked through the evening's events. What had possessed them to go there? The answers would have to wait until the next day when McKenzie's head had cleared enough to talk about it. However, another unfortunate side effect was that after the drug wore off, users sometimes found themselves unable to remember what happened while under its influence. They could feel woozy, hung-over, confused, dizzy, sluggish and uncoordinated, often with an upset stomach.

Otis said to Mary Jo, "Tomorrow isn't going to be pleasant for McKenzie. It's a good thing she's here for you to take care of. What a mess."

*****

In the morning, Otis went over to McKenzie's house to take care of Goldie, knowing McKenzie wouldn't be stirring for a while. He went to his office and came back home about eleven, when Mary Jo was trying to get some nourishment in McKenzie. She clutched her coffee cup as if it was the most precious thing she had ever touched. He and his assistant had already brought McKenzie's car back from the bar, and he would deal with the bartender and the druggers later.

"Okay, tell me what you remember and why you girls went to that place. Who were you looking for?" Otis asked.

"Ohhhh, my head hurts. I'm so sorry Otis, I didn't think it would be so scary. I just wanted to talk to this guy."

"What guy?" Otis demanded.

"The guy who lives in Frogtown, Dario somebody," she said, "he was playing pool."

"Dario. Dario who, and how do you know this guy?" Otis prodded.

"Oh, I don't really know him – I just wanted to talk to him – about my dad. I found out he was one of those guys who was being mean to the drivers at the trucking company. You know, what's the name?"

"Oh boy, I think you're trying to say Ward Transport – the company you happen to own, remember that one?"

"Yeah, I don't feel so good, please don't yell at me."

Mary Jo looked sideways at her husband and said, "Back off a little Otis, let's give her some space. I think she's petty queasy."

"I'm really sorry. I'm not thinking very straight just now and I guess I wasn't thinking very straight last night either. Oh, please don't tell Ethan what I did, please Otis? I can't let him find out what I did. I'd be so embarrassed." By this time McKenzie was crying and Mary Jo had her arms around her and was looking daggers at Otis.

Knowing when he was defeated, Otis decided to go back to the office and track down Colton and Trey; at least he had eventually gotten the names from Davey's bartender. He also had alerted the county sheriff to what had happened. The bartender admitted he didn't trust those two from the beginning but had never seen them do anything like that before. True or not, Otis would find them and find out what happened. He knew there were DFSA's being used in the Twin Cities, but he hadn't yet personally had to deal with any instances of their use. This needed to be nipped in the bud before it went any farther than it had already.

Kissing Mary Jo and leaving McKenzie in her care, he went off to talk with the sheriff and deal with the nasty business of not just finding Colton and Trey, but learning where they got their stash. Kenzie should be better the next day and they would start over then.

*****

The day was short with naps and bathroom trips, and McKenzie finally made it home. She called Janice to learn she wasn't faring any better than she was and apologized profusely. Janice was amazingly forgiving and McKenzie was grateful.

"We didn't find out anything about this Dario guy, but I think you're right and you should leave it in Otis's hands for now, okay?" Janice ventured.

"For sure," McKenzie agreed, "I don't want to try that again. I'm just glad we got out of there when we did. I'm not ready yet to tell Ethan about it, so I'd be grateful if you could keep this to yourself."

"Are you kidding?" Janice said in a whispered shout, "I don't want *anybody* to know how stupid we were. I'm not even telling Vicky. Consider it a done deal and we'll chalk that one off to experience – make that *bad* experience."

"Thanks, my friend. I'll try to find a safer adventure for next time." Before saying goodbye, they agreed that Deep Lake bars were a better place to meet for an occasional drink after this misadventure.

McKenzie saw that Ethan had tried to text her several times and he was getting worried. She called him to say she wasn't feeling well and thought she had caught some sort of bug. He was sorry for her and agreed she should stay home and rest for the evening.

Fortunately, she hadn't made any appointments for showing houses that day and was glad she hadn't stood up any potential clients. She took a slow stroll with Goldie and went back to the house for an early bedtime. It had been a lost night and day, she admitted to herself, and one she surely regretted. She couldn't afford to let this happen again.

CHAPTER 23
SHADY DEALINGS

The next day dawned brighter, and McKenzie welcomed her morning run. Goldie accompanied her now, and they both looked forward to the exercise and the time together. McKenzie tried to vary her pattern of running after her narrow escape with the pickup. It was both to deter anyone who might be watching for her for whatever intent, and also to give her the chance to check out different neighborhoods in the city. So much had changed through the years she was away, and she enjoyed the opportunity to look around her hometown. She saw areas that looked prosperous, where people had great pride of ownership in keeping up their homes. She also saw areas that weren't so well-kept, like the one she was running through at that moment. Some houses needed painting, some garbage cans were tipped over, and some yards needed mowing.

She was always on the lookout for houses that might be going up for sale no matter what area they were in. She was beginning to build up a clientele of people. She wanted to help find homes that worked for them, and found it satisfying to succeed. It wasn't just satisfying, it was downright fun for her to connect the right buyer with the right seller, and she had surprised herself that her new career had so quickly built that satisfaction. Getting to know the people was the first part of finding home-selling clients. Most of her contacts had come through the church because she continued to attend services weekly and stayed for coffee afterward to chat. Caring about each other was the amazing quality she had picked up on in the small-town atmosphere, and it was gratifying to see. People were concerned about their privacy as they were everywhere, but she saw concern for neighbors' well-being in Deep Lake, and it was comforting to her.

A few minutes before, McKenzie ran through her brother William's neighborhood with its well-kept and beautiful big homes. She was surprised to see Dolly out taking care of her own flowers as she thought most of the people in that area had someone else tending their yards. Dolly was wearing long sleeves and a big hat to protect her from the sun and the bugs, and it was obvious that she knew the plants in her garden. McKenzie assumed Dolly wouldn't appreciate company when she wasn't looking her best, so she just waved and called out a greeting as she ran by. Dolly straightened briefly and gave a half-hearted wave. McKenzie thought briefly of hope that their relationship could improve as time went on and vowed to help that happen.

However, when she was already past their neighbor-hood, McKenzie's remembered the warning about watching William. "William is self-involved and egotistic, and always has been," she thought, "but I just can't believe he would do anything to hurt our dad. Would he?" she continued to reflect and wondered how she could even talk about it with him. She needed to discuss with Otis about how to confront William and promised herself to do it soon.

At home after her run, she made a date with Ethan for that evening and planned to tell him about her misadventure with the scary guys and the Roofies. She dreaded the discussion but knew she couldn't hide this from someone she cared so much about. She worried about how he would take hearing what she had to say and hoped he wouldn't feel betrayed by what she had done.

She then reluctantly called Otis to thank him again for rescuing Janice and herself from what was certainly the result of a bad decision on her part, and about having a conversation with William. She first assured him she had recovered from the Roofies, and before she could bring up the question about her brother, Otis told her what had transpired with the whole situation at Davey's Bar. Colton and Trey had been caught and admitted to using the drugs and that was just the beginning.

The sheriffs of several counties were meeting with the governor and other state leaders to strategize on how to deal with the hard evidence that date-rape drugs were now being used in not just the metro area, but the suburbs of the Twin Cities, and how they were infiltrating into the rest of the Midwest. Knowingly, or unknowingly, McKenzie seemed to be at the hub of some grave and threatening issues in her new home. That sort of catalyst she never expected to be, but now that she was in the middle of it, she wanted to do anything she could to help.

Otis said he had already given his testimony about what happened with Janice and McKenzie, and after that he wasn't involved in the meetings that day. He was free again to work on his own priorities. At this point, his first priority was to find the killer of James Ward. "Oh Kenzie – you're so lucky you got out of there without anything worse happening. What made you think you could take off on your own after an obviously scary guy?"

"I just wanted to find out what happened to my dad. Surely you can understand that," McKenzie sheepishly replied.

"Of course, I understand. From here on, please let me know when you get another hair-brained idea and I'll go with you – if only to pick up the pieces."

"I hear you," McKenzie agreed. Thinking ahead and to get his mind off her appalling blunder, she added, "Have you done anything about checking out the guy that Dad fired from the trucking company?"

"I haven't yet," Otis admitted, "but I did get his name and address. The guy is Chuck Nelson, a harmless sounding Minnesota name if there ever was one. He lives in Apple Valley. This drug business is in the hands of the proper authorities now, and I'm ready to tackle this one. Actually, I was thinking of going over there today. You're welcome to come along – if you can hold yourself down and don't go off getting yourself in trouble.

McKenzie didn't have appointments for that day either, and said, "I'd love to go along – and I promise I'll behave – well a little anyway," she grinned, knowing Otis would forgive her no matter what she did.

"We'll head that direction and see what we see. I don't know if this guy is working now or not, or if he's even home. We'll check out his house anyway and maybe even talk with this man who was fired by James. I appreciate your instincts, and this could be an important contact."

In less than an hour, Otis picked her up in his squad car. McKenzie hoped her neighbors were watching and liked the idea of having the squad car in the neighborhood now and then. It made her feel safer and she hoped it worked on the neighbors, too.

On the way to Apple Valley, about thirty miles away, Otis filled her in on the details he got from Ed Johnson. Chuck Nelson had worked for Ward Transport for about two years. He was a problem from the beginning with unexplained absences and delayed deliveries, and as time went on, parts of loads began to disappear, a box here and a carton there were unaccounted for and customers began to complain. Johnson talked about it with James because Ed didn't want to hurt the guy's reputation by outright firing him. James eventually decided that was the only option and he did the firing himself. After Nelson left, a number of other issues came to light and everyone realized the man had been stealing much more than they were aware of at the time. James was the one who had dealt directly with Nelson in the altercation, and Nelson knew he was a judge. James had sternly told Nelson he was getting off lightly because he knew he was a family man, but he would be closely watching his actions in the future.

Watching Nelson in the future was the statement that worried Otis and McKenzie now. Did Nelson take drastic action to ensure James's inability to watch his actions? It was a frightening thought and one that must be followed up. McKenzie was anxious and a little bit scared they might be confronting her father's killer and she didn't know what reaction she might have.

Otis pulled up in front of a very large and gorgeous house in a good neighborhood. A huge and luxurious boat was in the driveway. It was more like a yacht, McKenzie thought, and the upper deck was loaded with canvas bags and boxes of supplies or something. The name on the side of the boat was 'Snow B Gone' and it looked like it was ready and waiting for some wonderful new adventure.

Otis made note of the boat and the house and looked at her with raised eyebrows. "Nice digs, don't 'cha think?"

They walked up the curved sidewalk and rang the bell. It was answered by a beautiful young woman in jeans. She was immediately agitated and seemed put off by Otis in his officer's uniform. He introduced himself and McKenzie, and the young woman said in a strong South American accent, that she was the au pair. Both Mr. and Mrs. Nelson were not at home and she was watching their two young children. They could see the children who were quietly watching TV in the family room just in sight of the front hallway. The young woman let Otis and McKenzie come into the front hallway but did not offer them a seat. Otis questioned her a little further in an official-sounding tone, but the girl didn't know where the Nelsons were and didn't know where or even if Mr. Nelson worked. She reluctantly gave them the cell phone numbers for both of the parents.

Otis asked the girl if the Nelsons were going on a trip. She didn't want to answer and finally said she had been helping them pack, but wasn't going with them. She didn't give any indication of what she would do when they left. She was obviously greatly relieved when Otis indicated he and McKenzie were leaving.

Back in the car, Otis and McKenzie started to discuss their feelings about the encounter, but the au pair was furtively peeking out the window at them and Otis decided to drive away.

"It looks like we've got another interesting situation here, Kenzie. What are your thoughts?"

"Interesting is right," she replied. "Somehow, I don't think this is the home of your average truck driver, to be honest. And that young woman seems more scared than she ought to be. I'd sure like to know the details of how she came to be here in this country."

"So would I, and that's what I'm going to try to find out. Excuse me because I've got to make a couple of calls right away." Otis parked the squad car a block away and called the Dakota County Sheriff's office as he didn't have jurisdiction outside of Washington County and this needed to be handled immediately. He suspected the au pair would be calling the Nelsons right away to tell them the police were asking questions, and the whole setting was suspicious. The sheriff agreed to send someone to watch the house so no one left the premises until they could get the situation checked out.

The next call was to the local Apple Valley police and he told them of the possibility of Nelson's connection to a potential homicide, and that he would meet with them as soon as he could get to their headquarters. "Hang on, Kenzie, I didn't know we'd be getting into another brouhaha so quickly, but I need to talk to these folks before Nelson has the chance to leave town. From the looks of that boat, it's an immediate possibility and I want to know what's going on with this guy. You're here now and there's not time to take you home, so I hope you're okay with going along."

"You bet I am! This could be the guy who killed my father and I'd do anything I can to make sure he pays for what he's done!"

Out of sight of the house, Otis turned on his siren and light bar in order to get to the police station as quickly as possible. Once there, McKenzie waited in reception while Otis talked with detectives about their suspicions. He learned that Nelson hadn't yet come home, but officers were waiting and they believed they had enough information to bring him to the station for questioning, if only as a person of interest. The wasp-sting death was unusual and those hearing the details were curious. When they heard Otis's description of the potential crime and ideas about how it could have happened, he saw nods throughout the room. It was becoming real to listeners that this could almost be the perfect murder. Each of them was already eager to find out if Nelson did it and if so, how. Officers were ordered to search around the house and grounds for wasp nests or activity, just in case.

Discussions with all of the authorities involved had taken several hours and at one point McKenzie was asked into the room to share her thoughts and observations. She was back in the waiting room and excitement had eased into exhaustion while Otis finished up. He finally came to get her and said he would handle things from that point on and work with the proper powers to deal with whatever Nelson had done or not done. Otis would take her home and go back to Apple Valley when they brought Nelson in so he could be there to see the look on his face when they started questioning him about James's murder.

McKenzie realized she didn't even want to see Nelson and she was grateful to go home. She had remembered that her dinner and confession to Ethan was only a couple of hours away and anxiety about all of that was setting in again. "What a day!" she thought with a sigh. "Could this be the answer to my father's death – at last?"

CHAPTER 24

CONFESSING TO ETHAN

McKenzie couldn't get into the shower fast enough to cleanse herself of the day's activities. While clean and orderly in appearance, Chuck Nelson's house itself had felt overpowering with a sense of deceit. The fear on the face of the au pair was nakedly evident when she saw Otis in uniform, and McKenzie felt frightened for the girl as well as for the children in her care. Tensely waiting all afternoon in the Apple Valley police station wasn't exactly pleasant either, and added to her feeling of grime.

What would come of the whole Nelson situation was exhausting to think about and she used her shower as the opportunity to wash away the anxieties and fears of her day.

Dressed simply in a relaxed skirt and top, and wearing sandals, she opened the door at Ethan's gentle knock, and melted into his arms. They hadn't seen each other for two days and at this point in their relationship, it felt like a month.

Breathing in her very essence, he said emotionally, "Oh, it feels so good to hold you. You smell like heaven itself and feel even better."

She smiled and closed her eyes in his embrace and rejoiced in his love. Their plan for the evening was to go to what had become their favorite spot, a restaurant with a great deck on the St. Croix River in Stillwater. But realism set in and McKenzie knew she had to first tell Ethan in a more private setting about what had happened on Dale Street. She pulled him into her living room and they sat across from each other on love seats in a cozy corner.

"Ethan, I have a difficult story to tell you and I'm afraid you'll be upset. First, please know I didn't mean to deceive you. It might look that way to you, but I'm afraid I didn't use good judgment when I planned this whole humiliating escapade."

Ethan's face showed concern as he sank down in his seat, and he said anxiously, "What did you do, Kenzie?"

McKenzie told the whole story and bravely left nothing out including her own serious lack of good judgment about trying to confront a potential killer. The resulting Roofie drug fiasco was hard for her to tell about but tell she did. Ethan sat listening quietly and when she told the worst parts, he closed his eyes and slowly shook his head.

She also included the information about her trip with Otis to confront Chuck Nelson. She was crying by the time she finished, because of her belief they had finally identified the man who murdered her father.

"Oh Ethan, I have to tell you that in the midst of all the horror surrounding my father's death, I'm almost relieved instead of feeling vengeful or hostile or anything like that, to think we've found the man who I really think killed my dad. He had the motive, with my father threatening to watch him for future illegal activities, and I believe he figured out the horrible means to do it. He's smart, but he's a terrible man and both Ed and Dad didn't realize how bad he was. I just know it!"

"So you really think he did it? What does Otis say about it?"

McKenzie had to admit that it hadn't yet been verified that Nelson did the killing, but she was so certain he had done it. She blurted, "It had to be him. It just had to!" She burst out crying again and almost screamed, "I was so afraid it was William who killed Dad!"

"William? What do you mean?"

"William has been so secretive since I've been home, and he never wanted to talk about Dad. He was so bitter about what happened with the company and Dad's will. When the FBI man said we should be looking at William, I froze inside. I was afraid to confront him about it and have been dreading even seeing him. Now that we've found out about this Nelson guy, I just know he's the one who did it and now I can't wait to see William to heal whatever has been wrong in our relationship."

When she finished her devastating story, Ethan looked up and again shook his head. He then took her hands in his and said softly, "What can I say, my dearest McKenzie, except that I am so sorry you have endured such devastating pain. You have not deceived me at all – it is I who haven't supported you as much as I should have. I know you have been upset and worrying about what happened to your father, but I blame myself for not understanding how truly tormenting this has been for you. I didn't realize to what lengths you would have gone in pursuing your instincts. I thought you were leaving this in the hands of professionals like Otis."

It was her turn to shake her head, "I couldn't, Ethan. I don't know what it is that makes me try to do everything on my own – I've been like that my whole life. I'm curious and I want to know why things happen the way they do. I want to know what makes people do what they do, and why they feel the way they do. I'm hopeless."

Ethan gave a laugh, "You're not hopeless, Kenzie, you're you. Nothing is going to change that, and I most certainly will never try to change you. I guess I didn't know the extent of your curiosity. It makes me wonder how much more I don't know about you, but that only deepens my love and strengthens my resolve to find out. That's the bottom line, McKenzie Ward. I love you now and I can only guess how much more I will love you as our future plays out together."

McKenzie squeaked, "Oh Ethan," and her tears increased to the point of blubbering. They finally looked at each other and laughed.

Standing, Ethan took her in his arms again, "You're safe now, my darling. I thank God you came through your adventure safely and I thank you for telling me what happened. As long as we have that honesty between us, nothing can drive us apart."

"Thank you for understanding. I don't know why I couldn't tell you before, but I am so grateful for your confidence in me and in our love. We're here and we're together, and may it always be so."

Their kiss was tender and healing and they stood in their embrace for several minutes. Suddenly, the sound of McKenzie's stomach growling interrupted the silence and they both broke into laughter. Ethan said, "Well, it sounds like dinner is calling. Let's find something to eat and talk about what's to come." After McKenzie fixed her tear-stained face, they left for Stillwater.

CHAPTER 25

CONFRONTATION

McKenzie heard from Otis that investigators were still working with detainee Chuck Nelson and were discovering several instances of fraud and even blackmail besides the thievery in which he had been involved. Otis called him "a nasty piece of work." The authorities had not yet really dug into what happened with her father, so she just had to wait, frustrating as it was.

She shared with Otis her conviction that Nelson had killed her father or had someone do it for him, and Otis listened patiently. He responded, "As I said before, we have to wait until the specialists do their jobs. I agree it looks like he was bitter enough to want to get back at James, but we can't prove anything yet. Please be patient."

"I'll try, Otis. I just want this to all be over and let my family be in the clear."

While waiting, she had a couple of days to do real work on her real estate activities and had listed two new houses to sell, which gave her new enthusiasm. She knew it was her responsibility to contact William about the recent developments, so, using her re-energized gusto she decided to call her brother. Her relief at what she saw as concrete evidence that William had nothing to do with their father's death, was incredibly freeing and she felt positively giddy. In her mind, Chuck Nelson was the culprit.

Unfortunately, William wasn't at home when she called, so she gave Dolly the message for William that something extremely important had come up and she needed to talk with him right away about their father's death. Dolly seemed to be very concerned with the call from McKenzie and asked, "What sort of information have you found out, McKenzie? Surely you can share it with me."

"No Dolly, I need to talk with William alone, so please have him call me," and McKenzie ended the call.

Waiting again for William to call, she decided to stay home that day to look at some of the things in the hidden storage areas of her house and garage. For the most part, it would give her something to do while she waited. She had ignored those areas for too long and believed it was time she did something with the many items her parents had left behind. Fired up with passion, she put on her grubbies and went out to tackle the attic of the old carriage house. Climbing the sharply vertical stairway to the attic, she saw trunks lining the walls and other items that were tossed here and there. Several pairs of old cross-country skis and boots were up there, and back in a corner was the baby bassinet including the yellowing lace that had cradled her own tiny self so long ago. Memories enveloped her as she poked around, still hesitant to open the boxes and feeling like an intruder.

She heard someone at the door of the garage and Goldie barked once, which was odd. "I'm up here," she yelled from the attic in a preoccupied voice, while digging through one of the trunks. She had found her father's old uniform from when he was in the Civil Air Patrol in high school. Knowing nothing about his experiences from those days, she wished now that her father had written a memoir or kept a more formal journal

… maybe there was something like that in these boxes, she thought and kept digging.

Forgetting about somebody being at the door, she was unexpectedly surprised when up popped Dolly who was climbing the steep attic stairs. Dolly had grabbed a hockey stick that was leaning against the stairs. McKenzie had tossed it down earlier thinking maybe William might want it.

Suddenly McKenzie looked at Dolly's face and saw not the perfectly groomed and turned-out Dolly she had always known, but a contorted sneer of sheer hatred. Shocked and bewildered, she cried out, "What?" just as Dolly viciously swung the hockey stick at her head.

McKenzie ducked her head to the side not a moment too soon and the stick hit her hard in her left upper arm, causing a bloody gash in her bare arm as well as a cruel bruise.

"You bitch!" Dolly shouted. "Now it's your turn!"

"What are you talking about, Dolly? I've never done anything to hurt you." McKenzie scrambled away from the stairway and fell backward on the floor in shock. In doing so, she realized she had her cell phone in her back jeans pocket, stuck there at the last moment before going to the garage, in case William called. Using her right hand, she pulled it out and behind her back pressed speed-dial buttons, praying she got them right.

Dolly was filled with rage and didn't seem to realize she was still standing on the top step of the ladder-like stairway. She waved the hockey stick around menacingly as McKenzie tried to scramble farther away. "It's *my* company," she yelled. "Mine! Your stupid grandfather stole it from my grandfather and it should have come to me!"

In her rage as well as seething arrogance, she told McKenzie that she had killed Rose Ward sixteen years before because Rose had found out about Dolly's family and threatened to tell James. "Everyone thought it was an accident that the radio fell into the bathtub – well it was no accident – I had had enough of that woman's whimpering, and I pushed the radio into the tub. I went to the house to confront her and when I heard her in the bathtub, I did what had to be done.

"I killed James, too. One night I found a big wasp nest when I checked my flowers. It was almost dark and it was so easy to put the nest in the freezer with my garden gloves on. It only took a few minutes for those little buggers to go to sleep. No one would ever find out they were in James's tackle box. It was the perfect solution if I do say so myself.

"And now it's your turn, you sneaky bitch. How convenient that I found you up here. You're going to have a terrible fall down these stairs, poor thing. You didn't realize how dangerous it was and you fell and broke your neck." Dolly started advancing toward McKenzie. "Just wait until …"

McKenzie had been struck dumb while Dolly raved, and neither of them realized that Goldie had entered the garage. She had been napping in the yard while McKenzie was working in the attic. She had given one bark when Dolly started looking around for McKenzie and stayed on vigilant alert when Dolly went into the garage. After Dolly hit McKenzie with the hockey stick, Goldie silently climbed the wooden stairs as Dolly was ranting. Just as she started to move closer to McKenzie again, Goldie grabbed Dolly's ankle with her sharp teeth and clamped on. Dolly screamed in shock and pain, "Owww! Let go, you damn mangy dog!" and she began to kick at the dog while kneeling on the attic floor with one foot still on the step. Goldie then let go of her leg and leaped around Dolly and up the top step. She stood on the floor of the attic, snarling and barking up into the raging woman's face. Waving the hockey stick and screaming at the dog, Dolly suddenly lurched backward. She lost her footing on the rickety stairway and crashed to the concrete floor below. Exactly as she had foretold, a neck was broken in the fall, but unknown to Dolly, she herself was the victim of her own treachery.

At that very moment, Otis's screaming squad car skidded to a stop in the drive. Thanks to McKenzie's quick thinking, he had heard Dolly's entire rant on his cell phone. He raced into the garage.

*****

Late that day, a small assembly sat in disbelief and amazement in McKenzie's living room. McKenzie was there, a picture of abject grief, held gently but firmly by Ethan. Heroic Goldie sat at their feet. William had crumpled into a corner chair. Dolly's body had been taken away hours before by the coroner, and Otis was unfolding the information he had gained since the morning's confrontation in the garage.

He told them that a visit to Dolly's childhood home in St. Paul had brought the whole story to light. It turned out that Dolly was the granddaughter of Antonio Antonini, the man McKenzie and Otis pulled out of the ice back in 1992. Aside from Rose Ward's later discovery of the relationship, no one in the Deep Lake area ever learned of the connection to Dolly's family. After Rose's death and through the years, Dolly made sure it never came to be known.

Antonini was the illegitimate father of Maria, Dolly's grandmother, who was born in 1932. Maria lived with her mother, Valentina, in St. Paul's Italian section around west Seventh Street. Valentina had been fascinated with gangster activities in the St. Paul area. She filled Maria's head with romantic stories of Antonini's being associated with famous mafia figures, including Bonnie and Clyde and John Dillinger. Antonini's disappearance and murder were never solved and Valentina romanticized his role in her life and remembered him forever as a hero.

Maria married late to a man named Gino Parino, had several miscarriages, and finally had a son, Antonio, or Tony, born in 1974 and named after his grandfather. A year later, Maria had Donna Parino, called Dolly, when Maria was well into her forties. Maria told her cherished Dolly greatly embellished stories of her brave grandfather, Tony Antonini, who owned the trucking company in Deep Lake. He drove the famous gangsters around and provided vehicles for their robberies and other illegal activities. He did all this while making them sound like Robin Hood adventures, and him a hero. Maria also told Dolly that after Antonini disappeared, his heirs were cheated out of his trucking company by that terrible thief, Big Jim Ward.

Dolly grew up determined to one day get the company back. She learned all she could about the Ward family and eventually arranged to be in a place where she could meet William Ward. It didn't take long for beautiful, blond, and cunning Dolly to woo a love-struck William into marriage.

A few years into the marriage, somehow, Rose Ward found out about Dolly's background. Rose met with Dolly alone and told her she was going to expose her to William and James.

Before she could do it, Dolly sneaked into the house and killed Rose by tipping the shelf and dropping the radio in the bathtub while Rose was taking a bath. Dolly knew about the house's outdated wiring, and saw the chance to keep her family secret. Rose's death was ruled a tragic accident.

Time went on and Dolly got too eager to become the owner of the company she had been waiting for all her life. She kept waiting for James to die and when he continued to enjoy his retirement in good health, she got impatient.

Otis explained, "From what Dolly said in the call I overheard, and what Ethan and another bee and wasp expert have put together, this is what we think happened with James's death. Dolly did her own flower gardening at home and was familiar with the behaviors of wasps. She must have discovered what we think was a paper wasp nest in her yard. She remembered that James was allergic to stings and decided she was tired of his interference in their lives and wanted him gone.

One evening at sundown when William was out and the wasps were tucked away in their nest, Dolly captured the nest, probably putting it in a plastic bag. She knew the wasps would react to cold temperatures and become sluggish, so she put the bag in their garage refrigerator where no one would see it. I actually found a couple of squashed and crumbled frozen wasps still in there when I looked this afternoon. After a couple of hours, she must have slit the nest and maybe filled a jar with a bunch of lethargic wasps. She drove over to James's house and when everything was quiet, opened the unlocked garage door. There was his car ready for fishing the next day. She opened the hatchback and saw his tackle box. I'm thinking she dumped out the jar full of sleepy wasps into his tackle box and slammed the lid.

"The next morning when James left for fishing, he loaded up Goldie, drove out to Lake Elmo, and waited for his buddy, Jake Connor, a retired attorney friend who often joined him. He must have decided to get ready before Jake got there, and took out his tackle box. I can just see him eagerly opening the tackle box while wondering what the fish would be biting on that morning.

"Out streamed a mass of wide awake and angry paper wasps from their confined space in the tackle box, and James was immediately stung around his face and hands up to twenty times or more. The shock of the stings was more than he could bear, and he fell behind the car and wasn't able to reach the console, where he had stored his Epi-pen and cell phone. With eyes and throat swelling shut, his breath must have become more and more shallow as the venom spread. Before long, his breathing stopped.

"What we guess was about twenty minutes later, Jake pulled up next to James's car and found the grisly sight. He called 911 right away, and an emergency vehicle was there within minutes. However, try as they did with paddles and shots, James could not be brought around."

Silence filled the room after Otis finished his disclosure of the horrifying events that unfolded. Disbelief filled their minds, but the greatest shock was that it was all true.

It was also learned that Dolly's brother, Tony, was the owner of the dirty gray pickup, which Otis saw when he went to the Parino family home after Dolly's fiendish attack on McKenzie. Always protective of his little sister, when Dolly told Tony that McKenzie had returned to Deep Lake and was causing trouble for her, he took matters into his own hands. He was the one who called in the night and tried to run

McKenzie down. Otis believed that Tony was also responsible for whatever had happened with Ed Johnson's brakes. Tony was already in custody and charges would be filed the next day.

William was wretched and consumed by grief. He finally stood wearily and said quietly, "I know she hurt the dog. With her tail, Goldie brushed a vase off the table and it broke. Dolly was so angry, she cut the dog's foot with the pieces. I was shocked at what she did but I was too embarrassed to tell you. I'm so sorry." He then looked McKenzie in the eye and said, "I didn't know about Mom and Dad." He left the house without looking again at any of them.

McKenzie believed William truly had no idea what Dolly was up to all along, and in spite of how he had always treated her, she felt sorry for him. It would be his responsibility to tell his daughter about everything, and that wouldn't be an easy thing to do. Far from it, she thought. Poor Sophie.

In the midst of the horror and revulsion of everything that had transpired, McKenzie hoped perhaps it would be possible in the future for brother and sister to eventually develop a new relationship. It would have to transcend the lies and deceit that had followed them since Dolly came into their lives.

Exhausted by the telling, but ever the optimist he was, Otis closed his eyes after looking at McKenzie being tenderly held by Ethan. He heaved a major sigh in the silence of the room and said, "Welcome home, McKenzie Ward, we're glad to have you back in Deep Lake. Before you know it, it'll be time for the ice-fishing contest again. Wanna bet I catch the first fish?"

ABOUT THE AUTHOR

Danger in Deep Lake is a first novel by Gloria VanDemmeltraadt, writing as Gloria Van. The cozy mystery is set in a small town in rural Minnesota, not far from the metropolis of the state's Twin Cities. McKenzie Ward left Deep Lake years ago to charter a new course. When the successful New York Realtor learns of her father's strange death by bee sting, she returns home for answers. Many things have changed while some remain the same. Long buried secrets, submerged deep as the lake itself start to bubble up. They challenge McKenzie's memories of events and the people she thought she knew so well.

Other books:

Describing her own life experiences in a unique way, Gloria VanDemmeltraadt's first book, *Musing and Munching*, is both a memoir and a cookbook. Her work focuses on drawing out precious memories. As a hospice volunteer, she continues to hone her gift for capturing life stories and has documented the lives of more than a hundred patients. She refined this gift in *Memories of Lake Elmo*, a collection of remembrances telling the evolving story of a charming village.

Gloria continues her passion to help people capture their life stories, and has brilliantly caught the essence of her husband's early life in war-torn Indonesia. The paradise of the Dutch East Indies was shattered when Japanese storm troopers poured over the island of Java in March 1942. In *Darkness in Paradise*, Onno VanDemmeltraadt's story is touchingly told amid the horrors of war. This work has been praised by Tom Brokaw and has also earned the New Apple Award for Excellence in Independent Publishing for 2017 as the Solo Medalist Award for Historical Nonfiction.

The theme of legacy writing continues with her fourth nonfiction book, a clear and concise how-to manual called *Capturing Your Story, Writing a memoir step by step*. The book capsulizes information shared in numerous classes Gloria has given within the wider Twin Cities area on how to capture personal memories to write a simple collection of stories for family, or as a memoir to be published.

Gloria lives and writes in mid-Minnesota. Contact her through her website: **gloriavan.com**

CPSIA information can be obtained
at www.ICGtesting.com
Printed in the USA
LVHW050919190119
604509LV00034B/1191/P

9 780990 837503